D1487597
DISCARD

# Bells will, be Ringin

# MICHELLE MITCHELL

Copyright © 2017 by Michelle Mitchell

All rights reserved.

No part of this book may be reproduced in any form or by any electronic or mechanical means, including information storage and retrieval systems, without written permission from the author, except for the use of brief quotations in a book review.

# Acknowledgment

Thank you Lord for another chance to share this gift with others. And thank you so much to my family for being so crazy, and for the love and laughter.

To Rhonda McKnight and Sherri Lewis, thank you for your support, your guidance, and the helpful feedback you provided to bring this project to life. You are two amazingly talented women.

To the Mitchell family, I love our family and all of the memories that we share. I will forever have laughter in my life because of all we've been through as a family.

To my cousin, Sharita Haskins, thank you for skipping out on mandatory nap times and plotting to take over the play kitchen. We had way too many sleepovers and adventures to count. And to Allen, thank you for introducing me to the phrase "wormy and creamy" when I think about hot cocoa.

To Felicia Roberts and Kisha Dodd, thanks for being ready to fight for me and with me when someone thought I was trying to steal their boyfriend.

To Urshla Roberts-Jackson, thanks for sharing Uncle Tommy with us and always being ready to laugh. To my cousin Rhonda, thanks for riding me around in your Eclipse. I use to love that car.

To Terance and Jerrold Kilgore, and Thomas Roberts, thanks for giving me the fear of Jason Voorhees and Freddy Krueger—it's because of you I'll never know what happened on Elm Street and will continue to avoid Friday the 13th at all cost.

To Trina Reid and Marlon Blount, thank you for living in a neighborhood with a candy lady. They didn't have that in Kennesaw. And I can't forget about you Kaliba a.k.a, Lelee—you were a sweet baby and now I'm so proud to say that you're an amazing woman.

To Niecia Reynolds and Drika Dodd, thanks for Loca Luna—that's all I'll say about that. I can't forget about Carvin and Eric Dodd, thanks for giving me a Cowboys fan to heckle and so many childhood memories.

To Magic and Sirone Mitchell, thanks for freestyling in the car with me and helping prove that I had better bars. And thanks for maintaining your sense of humor all these years, some of my favorite childhood memories included you two.

And to the rest of my cousins, thank you for every moment we have shared old and new. I love you guys with everything in me.

And thank you to the readers, those that have me a chance with my debut novel, *Truth Is...* and those that are coming back to see what I have to offer this time around. Thank you for reading and coming along on this journey with me.

Email: authormichellemitchell@gmail.com
Facebook: www.facebook.com/AuthorMichelleMitchell
Twitter: https://twitter.com/expbutterflies
Instagram: www.instagram.com/authormichellemitchell

**Dedicated to the Mitchell Family**

# Table of Contents

# Chapter 1

I sprinted through the Dallas Fort Worth International Airport determined to make my flight. I woke up late. The story of my pillow-clutching life. I regretted my attire. I wore heels that pinched my feet, black compression leggings meant for the gym, and then there was the poorly buttoned, black and yellow flannel top that clung to me as I hurried through the mass of holiday travelers. I'm pretty sure I clipped a few people with my duffle bag and rolled over a few toes. I spewed a few aimless apologies and kept it moving to my gate.

I should've been in my seat already, but the spat I had on the phone with Charles, my boyfriend of five years, had put a dent in that plan. He drove me crazy—in more ways than one. I loved him, and only wanted to be with him, but he wasn't great at balancing his time. Like right now, he should've been preparing to pick me up from the Hartsfield-Jackson Atlanta International airport upon my arrival, but no – it was more important for him to be with the partners at a cabin in Colorado.

Don't get me wrong. I was supportive of my man and would've loved for him to be the first black partner at his law firm, but I was also a big advocate for all things us. Every year, every Christmas, consisted of him schmoozing clients to impress the partners and not spending time with me. The holidays were major in my family, and neither one of us wanted to force the other to choose. But this Christmas, I wanted him to be there to support me as I walked into what might be a hornet's nest of drama with my siblings. I shook away my thoughts and returned my focus to the holiday hustle and bustle of the airport.

The announcement of reminders about not leaving unattended bags and changes in departure made my heart race at the same speed as my feet as I hurdled over bags and did spin moves that could've gotten me drafted by any NBA or NFL team. Determined not to miss my flight, I picked up my pace. My ankles burned and my calves were going to be killer after this workout, but it was worth it once I got to my destination.

I managed to get to the gate right as they were boarding the last zone. Considering I would be the last to board, I was glad I decided to check the majority of my luggage. I was sure the overhead bins were near full by now, but I was going to make my duffle bag fit one way or the other.

Running my fingers through my short, coily hair, I hustled down the narrow aisle to get to my seat. I'd spent a little extra to get some leg room. Being tall and traveling in cramped spaces, I had learned it was well worth the investment.

I looked down at my seatmate, who had his earbuds in and hadn't noticed I was looming in the aisle waiting to sit down.

"Excuse me. Would you mind letting me in?"

"Oh, I'm sorry. Here, let me get up so you can get by."

He smiled as he rose, and I noticed a slight snaggletooth. Taking in his burly frame, I assumed he played football at some point in his life. Average looking guy.

"Thank you," I said, as I settled into my seat.

Out the corner of my eye, I continued to study him. Probably much longer than what was socially acceptable, but I had watched one too many ID channel marathons to drop my guard. As he turned his head in my direction, I gave a fake smile and waited for the airplane banter to commence. My flight routine consisted of boarding, reading, and sleeping. I hoped this chat would prove him to not be crazy so I could relax.

"So you going to Atlanta to visit or that's home?"

"Home," I replied. "I was here for a three-day National Association of Realtors Conference and Expo."

Real estate was a career I stumbled into after attending an open house with my friend Keesa Swain, who spent years working in real estate before getting her license to be a broker. I had always had an interest in interior design and helped Keesa stage the houses she sold. Once Keesa told me she wanted to start her own real estate agency, I took the steps toward getting my real estate license. That was two years ago, and we'd been working together ever since. Around Atlanta, we had been christened as Queens of the Hunt, because we found our clients the home of their dreams.

"Oh, ok. Commercial real estate?"

"No, I'm in residential real estate," I replied. "What do you do?"

I had to take his focus off me. Before I told him anything further, I needed to see if he was a contact worth making. I wasn't risking my life for some clown who wasn't in the market for a home and had the potential of stalking me for sport. No thanks. He would not be collecting my skin today.

"I'm a scout for the Atlanta Falcons, and I'm Felix, by the way. I was out here following up on some prospects at the Frisco Bowl."

My eyes widened. "Oh wow...I'm Harper, probably your new best friend. My family is full of die-hard Falcon fans. With the exception of my mother. She was misguided as a child and cheers for the Saints. It's always interesting in our house when we play them."

Felix guffawed. "I bet. It's like that in my family too, but we're split between the Packers and the Bears."

This time I laughed. "Oh yeah, that's some beef right there." I nodded as I made a mental note to give him my card. "Well, I won't continue to chew your ear off. I'm about to plug in these ear buds and catch up on some reading. Once I get to my mother's house, there'll be no rest and relaxation for me."

He nodded and reclined his seat. Guess he wanted a reprieve, too.

As I flipped through the pages of *Sister Surrogate* by LaChelle Weaver, I thought about my siblings and the tension awaiting me once I got to my parents' house. This time last year, I got way too involved in my sister, Wesleigh, and my brother, Donovan's, lives. I got it honest though, because my mother always said as the big sister, I should work towards helping them grow by leading as a good example.

So when my sister was about to make a huge career decision without doing her research, I stepped in and managed to disrupt what she still to this day believes was the opportunity of a lifetime. Then there was my brother, Donovan, who was so in love with his now ex, Paula. She wasn't right for him, but I couldn't allow him to figure it out on his own.

Now they're both upset with me for getting too involved, and my mother blames me for ruining Christmas since it all blew up right there during our annual Christmas Eve dinner. I get it, but it was my mother who always wanted me to get involved in their lives and overplay the big sister role. It's not my fault I was trained to be the dream killer.

I gave up on my book, reclined my seat and closed my eyes. The more I thought about seeing my family, I realized this might be the most peace I would have for the next few days.

Two hours later, my newfound friend Felix and I were both waiting for our bags in the baggage claim area. I pulled out my phone to request an Uber to take me to my house. Charles drove me to the airport for my trip to Texas, and since he changed our plans, I now needed a way home.

I looked over and saw Felix on his phone. My plan was to get his card and some of his NFL contacts. Football players needed a home and I needed to make a sale.

"Felix, thanks again for everything. Can I get your card? Here's mine. I'd love to help you or some of your new recruits, *ahem*, find a new house," I offered.

He pulled out his wallet and retrieved a card. "Thanks. That would be great. I do have a few recruits I hope to sign here soon, so this works out great."

As he began to walk toward the exit, I extended the handle on my bag and rolled out right behind him. As I looked for my Uber driver, who was supposed to be in a midnight blue, Jeep Grand Cherokee, I saw a beautiful redhead step out of the car to meet Felix. The glacier on her left hand let me know she was his fiancée. I needed to say hello. Maybe they needed a house, too. New wife, new beginnings…it was a no brainer really.

"Welcome home, baby," she greeted. He lifted her off the ground. They kissed. "How was your flight?"

"Good, but not as good as it is to see you. I missed you, girl," Felix said, planting a deep kiss on her lips and gripping her behind.

I looked away. I felt like I was violating their privacy. After they loaded the car, I hustled over to introduce myself.

"Excuse me, hi—I'm so sorry to interrupt. I sat by your fiancé on the flight and I couldn't help but notice this glacier you got on your finger. Congrats."

She squinted her eyes, studying me. I began smoothing out my wrinkled attire self-consciously.

Felix chuckled at the awkward exchange. "Meeghan, meet Harper Hilson. She's in real estate. I told her I might have a few rookies who might be interested in a home. I guess she thinks we might be in the market here soon, too."

Meeghan finally smiled in my direction. I guess the thought of buying a house changed her disposition She shook off whatever was on her mind and spoke. "Talk about divine intervention. God is so awesome," Meeghan squealed.

I smirked. Looking back and forth between Felix and Meeghan, I asked, "Did I miss something?"

"Oh, I'm sorry," Meeghan said, shaking her head. "I hadn't had a chance to tell Felix yet, but the offer we put on a home fell through. The appraisal came back lower than the seller was willing to go. So we're actually on the market—again."

"How unfortunate. I'm sorry to hear that, but I'd be lying if I didn't say I'd love to help you secure a home."

Meeghan put her arms around Felix's back, leaned in close, and looked up at him. "That's definitely something for us to consider, baby."

"Well, you might hear from us soon, Ms. Hilson," Felix said.

"Hilson?" She snapped her fingers. "You wouldn't happen to be related to Wesleigh Hilson, would you? I'm a member at her gym."

I smiled proudly. "Yes, that's my younger sister."

"Oh, super cool. Maybe I'll see you for one of her legendary spin classes in the near future."

I chuckled. "That's highly unlikely. I'm one and done."

They waved their goodbyes and turned to get into the car. As they drove away, my Uber driver pulled up.

"Hello. Sorry about that. It was crazy trying to get over here to you and you know Atlanta PD doesn't play about being parked out here," the young man, identified as Kwesi on the Uber app, said.

"No problem at all. I'm glad you were close by and my wait was minimal," I stated.

Sliding into the car, I leaned my head back on the seat and relaxed. I hoped I got to my mom's house before at least one of my siblings. The last one to arrive was always burdened with the undesirable Christmas tasks like untangling lights and sorting through tinsel and ornaments from Christmas past. The thought made me smile. In reality, I didn't care what I got assigned. I was just happy to be with my family for another holiday.

Try as I might to focus on the happier memories, I couldn't shake the nagging feeling that this would be a not so merry Christmas. After what I had done to my siblings, I had no clue what was waiting for me once I walked through the door. I squirmed in my seat, no longer feeling optimistic about returning home for the holidays. But no matter what happened, I resolved to keep my nose out of others people's business—at least for the rest of this year. No, period.

Yes sir, Harper Hilson's days of being nosey were over. From here on out, I would mind my business and only offer help if asked. Feeling confident about my decision, I sunk further into the seat and looked out the window. This year would be different. I could feel it.

# Chapter 2

My Uber driver was a cute little something. His curly-top fade, single dimple, and long lashes against his dark berry complexion were adorable. I looked at his reflection in the rearview mirror and noticed he had on a Morehouse sweatshirt. I bet the ladies of Spelman and Clark Atlanta swooned when they saw him on the yard.

"I see you're a Morehouse man. What year?"

He looked down at his chest. "Oh, nah. My dad went there and he's a professor there now. He keeps me geared up, but I'm in school at Georgia Tech."

"I bet that went over well. Was he disappointed?"

My father had graduated from the University of Georgia and wanted us all to be down with the Dawgs. But I graduated from Georgia Southern University, my younger sister went to Kennesaw State University, and my brother did a stint at Chattahoochee Tech before blowing up in the auto industry. My dad got over that once my brother got him his dream car—an electric blue Corvette. My mother had a fit when she saw that car in her driveway.

"Not really. I got an academic and basketball scholarship, so that trumped what he desired."

"I bet they're proud. Did your mom go to school in the Atlanta University Center as well?"

He nodded. "My mom went to Clark."

I beamed. "Aw, yes. The age-old tale of boy goes to college and meets girl that won't leave without an MRS degree. I ain't mad at it."

He chuckled. "Actually, they started dating in high school. I was their graduation gift."

Kwesi had to be about nineteen years old, if that. I assumed his parents were in their late thirties like me.

"Gotcha. Sounds like you were their motivation to continue and get that education, though. You said your father was a professor, right?"

"Yup. Dr. Jabari Morrison. He has a few books out there as well and does a lot of speaking engagements."

I felt my face flush. I knew this wasn't Jabari – my supposed-to-be-high-school-sweetheart-that-cheated-on-me-with-who-I-assume-is-this-kid's-mother – Morrison from my past.

"That's great." I waited a beat and then, "Uh, you sound super proud of your dad. And what about your mom? Is she in academia as well?"

"Nah, my mom is a claims adjuster."

I cleared my throat. "Awesome. Yeah, I thought I would've had the whole high school romance thing, too. I'm from around this area," I noted as we got closer to the house. "I went to McEachern High School and then went down South for college."

"Oh word. My parents went to McEachern, too. My mom's name was Terri Fordham and well, I told you my dad's name. You know them?"

I swallowed hard. "I believe I just might. Small world." I laughed awkwardly, pausing briefly to regroup. "It's great that your dad decided to give back to the school where he earned his degree. Do you mind turning on the radio? Preferably like Kiss 104 or Boom 97.5."

He pressed a button on his radio and the car filled with the sounds of Whitney Houston declaring someone gave her good love. The song made me think of Charles. That's who my thoughts should be on—not Jabari. Charles loved me deep, and I wanted him to give me more time. I didn't push the issue because I understood how important it was for him to become partner. I was trying to be patient, but I was ready for him to make us official. In order for that to work, there had to be some balance between his love for me and his love for his career.

Speaking of Charles, my phone chimed with a text from him.

*Charles: Hey pooh. Did you make it in okay? Call me when you get to the house. I texted you some pics of the cabins we are in this year. This place is even better than last year. Maybe one day you'll see it in person.*

*Harper: Yeah I'm here. In an Uber trying to get home since my boyfriend left me stranded. Enjoy your trip.*

I rolled my eyes. I would love to be in a cabin surrounded by snow with my man to keep me warm. It was Christmas though and I wanted to be around family, not a bunch of overworked attorneys who would spend the entire time drinking and talking briefs. No thanks.

We had yet to spend the holiday together. Christmas was my favorite holiday, and since he knew that, I wished he'd consulted with me first before making plans to attend this annual event. It wasn't like he couldn't miss one or two.

As we passed the sign indicating we were now in Downtown Powder Springs, I allowed myself to get caught up in memories of my childhood. After college, I moved to a Smyrna, which was only minutes away from my childhood home. Crossing over the railroad tracks, I smirked as I looked over at the cute, red brick storefronts where my friends and I would hang on weekends. I loved growing up here. A lot of great moments happened here.

Memories of Jabari crept in. I inhaled deeply. I hadn't heard the name Jabari in a minute. No, I was lying. I had Facebook stalked him for a second, but after seeing he and Terri were still happy, I stopped snooping. Not that I wanted them to be miserable, but on occasion I flashed back to high school. Back then, I thought Jabari and I would go from turning our tassels on graduation day to daydreams of us snapping photos of our child celebrating that same moment, but as husband and wife.

Jabari and I were voted "most likely to marry" in the senior superlatives. We were the homecoming king and queen. As far as I was concerned, it was written in the Lamb's Book of Life for Jabari and me to get married, but nope – that's not how it went down. No, instead it went down with Mr. Morrison in the library with the broken condom with Ms. Scarlett Letter, Terri Fordham. I was embarrassed and heartbroken when he told me she was pregnant with his baby.

We had made plans, plans he broke once he messed around with that skeezer Terri. She was always trying to one up me. If I got a new purse, she got a new purse and a new pair of shoes. I ran for student body president and she ran, too. There was always an unspoken rivalry between the two of us. And then finally, I had something she didn't—Jabari. But then she somehow managed to sway him. Or perhaps, I was blinded the entire time.

The car came to a stop, shaking me out of my thoughts.

"I'm gonna hop out and grab your bags from the trunk," Kwesi said.

I stepped out of the car and walked around toward the back to get a better look at him. I don't know how I managed to overlook how much he looked like his father when we were students at McEachern High School. There was pinch of Terri in there, too, but all the good parts were Jabari. I reached into my purse to grab a few bucks to tip him.

"Thank you, Kwesi. Have a Merry Christmas if I don't run into you—or *ride* with you again."

He chuckled and gave me a mock salute before getting back into the car.

I rolled my bag up to the front door of my three-bedroom, ranch style home and went inside. I sent my family a message to let them know I was home unpacking and would be by later. Our pre-Christmas Eve get together was in four hours. I had just enough time to shower and relax in front of a good book or the television. A nap was out of the question. I knew if I let my eyes close, my mother would see to it I never opened them again. She didn't stand for tardiness and she didn't understand the words, "I won't be able to make it" either.

The thought brought me back to Charles. That was an expectation I wished I could set with him. I no longer wanted to hear, "I can't make it" on the holidays or whenever the partners wanted him to be at their beck and call. I wasn't sure how I would do it, but before we went into the New Year, I had to figure out a way to get Charles to get onboard with more quality time. I wasn't sure how to make it happen, considering I was always so accommodating.

That had always been a problem for me. I was too much of a people-pleaser. My inability to speak up for myself was the sole reason Terri was able to scoop up Jabari, and why I never felt comfortable letting Charles know what I needed from him. That was about to change, or at least I hoped it would.

# Chapter 3

After freshening up from my post-flight nap, I loaded my gifts and two overnight bags into my trunk, and made my way over to my parents' house. The commute was only thirty minutes, but considering what was waiting for me, it felt a lot longer. My head raced and my heart percolated, as I pulled into the driveway. Getting out of the car, I looked up at the two-story, craftsman style home, and was instantly flooded with memories.

I put my key in the front door and turned the knob. I could hear the loud talking and music playing from the family room as soon as I stepped inside. I knew I was later than my mother would like, so I tried to slide in and find a way to merge into the group, but my loudmouth brother wouldn't let me be great.

"Oooh, Mama. Harp walking up in here late *and* empty handed," Donovan tattled.

I sucked my teeth and nudged him in the side. I had forgotten she sent me a text to get some aluminum foil and paper plates. Guess I'd be on dishwashing duty tonight.

My mother walked into the hallway where my brother and I were now engaged in his favorite game— slap boxing.

"Ugh, really Donnie? You always trying to tell on somebody," I said, smacking him across the top of his head.

"Harper Layne Hilson, you stop hitting your brother." A beat and then, "Are you okay, sweetheart?" She cooed over Donovan. You wouldn't know my brother was thirty years old and standing at six foot, two inches, he towered over my five foot even mother. The way she babied him, you would think she pushed him out of her womb this morning.

"Ma, he came at me first," I whined, crossing my arms over my chest. "That's not right. You don't even know who started it."

"I know how to finish it though. Oh and Harper, thanks for *getting* the foil by the way," my mother chided.

My mother was good for indirectly stating her disappointment. She enjoyed her sarcasm as much as she enjoyed quilting and sipping wine. She loved us equally though, but she had her moments where Donovan got a little extra love.

"Hey now. If it isn't Auntie's Split Pea. Come give me a hug," Aunt Ephranette said.

I rolled my eyes before turning to face my aunt Ephranette who walked out of the kitchen and joined us in the entryway. My mom and her sister, or as we called them, The Nettes, were both summed up in two adjectives – sarcastic and unfiltered. My mother, Lynette, was the baby in the group. Their brother, Lafayette, was just as bad. He was sarcastic, unfiltered, and loud enough to wake the dead.

"Hey, Auntie," I said. "How are you?"

"Better than you," she said giving me a sidelong look. "Chile, I know that little pea butt from anywhere," she said turning me around. "Ain't got no kind of butt back there. Definitely not from our side, you can thank your daddy's genes. Guess those peas won't ever swell up. Good thang you got these expired milk factories up here," she said squeezing my breast without warning. "Sure would be nice for you to give my sister some grandkids." A beat and then, "Let me go check on my cobbler, messing with you."

My eyes narrowed as I looked over at Donovan, who was laughing a little too hard at my expense. I was about to swing on him again when my mother's radar went off and her eyes bore into me, letting me know that as soon as I hit him, she was gonna hit me.

As soon as she turned the corner, I thumped him in the head and ran towards the kitchen behind my mother and aunt. My younger sister, Wesleigh was sitting at the island on one of the barstools peeling potatoes. Her long, fussy, black curls were pulled into a high bun on top of her head. The new, copper highlights in her hair brought out her gingerbread complexion. I swear she was a walking billboard for her gym.

"Well, it's about time y'all brought your lazy butts in here. I don't know how I got cast as Florence and y'all got to be Jenny and Lionel."

24

I chuckled. "This is not *The Jefferson's,* little sister, and you know all of us have chores."

Wesleigh tilted her head to the side. "Oh ok, so what are you and Donovan working on? Y'all look empty handed to me. The prep for cooking is pretty much done. I guess y'all should get to work on detangling the rest of those Christmas lights."

As soon as the word "detangle" came out of my sister's mouth, Donovan dipped from the room, leaving me with one of the worst tasks of all.

"That's a good idea, Wessy. Harper, honey, go ahead and get those lights out of the garage and start detangling."

I folded my arms. "Okay, and what is *Donovan* going to be doing? Or is he doing the dishes?" I said an octave higher to make sure he heard me.

He came flying around the corner. "I'll help with the lights. I just had to use the bathroom."

I grinned as he sneered at me. My plan worked. He knew as much as I did he would be doing that chore on his own. My idea of helping was to tangle the lights up more so he would relieve me of my duties. To this day, I don't think he ever caught on to my trickery. I considered it my little Christmas gift to him.

So far, I was glad to be here with everyone. My brother and sister appeared to be their normal playful selves and perhaps they weren't resentful anymore. The energy felt good. My eyes beamed at the thought of a drama-free Christmas.

My smile turned down as I saw aunt Ephranette's lips twisted up as she looked at me and my siblings.

"You know, it don't make no kind of sense you named these two girls' *boys'* names. What type of man wants to be with a woman named Harper or Wesleigh? Need to say they full names to give them some kind of femininity, Harper Layne and Wesleigh Rose. Now that sounds nice."

I cleared my throat. *"Anyway*, where is daddy at?"

"Right behind you, Baby Girl," he said before kissing me on my cheek. "'Bout time you got here."

Andrew Hilson was a retired mechanic. After a short-lived retirement, he decided he wanted to open his own repair shop. He'd had several customers tell him if he ever left his old job and opened his own place they would follow him. After sitting at home a month after retiring, he put a plan in motion with Uncle Lafayette, and business had been booming. Donovan was the shop manager.

After dad's business took off, Donovan had insisted they use the rest of the land the repair shop was on to sell used and new cars. Together, they made Hilson and Braggs Auto the preferred place for purchases and repairs.

"Now that everyone is here, are we gon' eat something around this place?"

"I think Mama said it'll be a few more minutes before the meatloaf is done."

Wesleigh got up from her seat and took the potatoes she was peeling over to the stove to place in the boiling water.

Dad threw his hands up. "Aw shoot, well I'm about to get some of this sweet potato pie to hold me over."

"Oh no you don't." My mom rushed over to swat his hands. "You can wait a few more minutes on the meatloaf. Eat some fruit or something."

My father spun on his heels and tickled my mother. "Well if I can't eat yet, then I might as well go work up my appetite. Get on up them stairs, girl—so you can do that thang I like."

"*Drew*...not in front of the kids," she gushed.

"Puh-lease not in front of the kids," I pleaded.

"Amen," Donovan and Wesleigh said in unison.

My father dismissed us with a wave of his hand. He reached into his pants pocket and pulled out his wallet. "Here, why don't y'all kids go get some ice cream or something?"

I took the money from his hands. "Um, Pop, what we gonna to do with six dollars?"

He ignored my question and began singing Marvin Gaye's "Sexual Healing" to my mother. "*And when Drew gets that feeling, Nette be serving me some sex-ual healing...*"

"Aww, heck nah," Donovan yelped, turning his head.

"*Take me to the king,*" I sang.

"Get thee behind me, satan," Wesleigh bellowed.

My mother guffawed at our antics. My father playfully snatched back his six dollars. "Y'all some ol' hatin' kids." He chuckled. "Make me sick. Bustin' up my groove. Y'all can get your own ice cream."

Donovan shrugged. "Ice cream can't undo what was done. I think we deserve to have our allowance reinstated."

"Facts," Wesleigh and I said in unison.

"I don't know how I managed to have three kids who don't have a lick of sense." He shook his head, laughing inwardly.

Aunt Ephranette huffed. "Sense ain't common. It's a blessing from God and it's clear He skipped right over these chilluns' y'all got over here."

My father's eyes widened before he broke into a hearty laugh. "On that note, I'm going back in here to watch television." He shook his head and walked out of the kitchen. My mother and aunt were not far behind.

Left alone with only my siblings and my thoughts, I decided to extend an olive branch.

"Wow…that's y'all daddy," I joked. "So uh…do y'all want to go get this ice cream? My treat."

Wesleigh didn't respond. Instead, she turned and walked out of the kitchen. I guess there was still some ice to be thawed with her. I didn't know why I was expecting this to be easy, but I also wasn't expecting her grudge to be so deeply rooted she wouldn't even join me for ice cream.

I didn't give up hope that my brother would take me up on the offer. I cleared my throat. "Donnie, what about you?"

He shrugged. "Nah. I'll take a raincheck. Maybe instead of trying to bribe us with a sweet treat, you should be asking to go somewhere to talk."

"I know. That's what I was trying to do—get out of the house and go somewhere where we could have fun and hopefully make peace."

He nodded. "Yeah okay, but you know good and well it would've been more focus on having fun than you actually apologizing to anyone."

"That's not true. I know you both are upset or were upset with me, and I want to make things right and talk about what happened last year. Let everyone get their feelings out there."

"Listen, I'm good. I just wish you would put more effort into fixing your own messes."

My brow raised. "I'm sorry…what are you trying to say?"

He pushed off the wall and walked closer to me. "I mean—where is Charles this Christmas? Didn't he say last year he'd definitely be present this year?"

I stood there speechless. Since we had been together, Charles had yet to attend or at least stay for the whole weekend of a Hilson family Christmas. I admit I was disappointed, but I understood what I was up against when it came to his career aspirations. I guess I let myself believe no one in my family was paying attention to this trend of his. Meeting Donovan's eyes, I blinked back tears as he patted me on my shoulder in passing—his point made.

# Chapter 4

I woke up in my childhood bed and stretched out to readjust my body. One wrong move on this full size bed and I was going to be lying on the floor. At least the pillows were firm. This bed used to feel much bigger back in my high school days.

The only new items in this room were the teal and beige linens on the bed. My dresser still had my cheerleading trophies, photographs from senior bonfires stuck in the attached mirror, and a few yearbooks. The mattress was due for an overhaul. I'd have to make sure to purchase one for this room. Not that my parents had company often, but it would be nice to do since I stayed here on occasion if out in the area or for holidays.

I rolled over again trying to find my sweet spot, when the smell of bacon cooking slapped me in the face. Bacon was my vice. I could eat it on everything and have tried. I've had chocolate covered bacon. Bacon and Frosted Flakes. Maple Bacon Cookies…I'd eat it with whatever, whenever and however.

I padded across the floor and crept downstairs to the kitchen. I hoped my siblings were still asleep. I wanted to get my bacon before everyone else put their little hands in there, touching everything. My brother was notorious for picking through food using his hands instead of a utensil. He was our own personal caveman.

"Good morn—*dang*. What are you doing down here?" I whined, when I saw Donovan preparing his plate.

"Do you see anyone else down here?" he replied. "I made breakfast for everyone. Grits with cheese on the side for y'all crazy folks, and sugar too. You know pop still puts sugar in his grits." He grimaced.

"Don't knock it. Daddy put me on and I'll admit it was swanging." I rubbed my belly and licked my lips.

Donovan smirked. "Yeah, whatever. I got some batter ready to drop some pancakes and waffles, and got some scrambled eggs, too. If you want to eat—you betta hit them dishes."

I shook my head. "I got you, but I'm going to eat first." I grabbed a festive, red paper plate with green Christmas trees on it from the package we would use later tonight. As I saw Donovan's eyes light up mischievously, no doubt prepared to tell on me, I intercepted his comment. "If you snitch on me, I swear I'm going to kick your behind. It's one plate. Don't make it a big deal."

He chuckled. "I wasn't going to say anything about a plate. I see something more amusing."

I looked down at my pajamas, an Atlanta Falcons tank top and matching flannel bottoms. I reached up and touched my satin scarf. "What's funny?"

He lifted his shoulders. "Nothing I plan to share. This is too good. I'm not giving up these goods."

There was a knock at the door. Donovan and I eyed each other. We were both determined not to move towards the door. A few seconds passed before our battle to see who could be the most stubborn was broken by another knock at the door.

"You best go get it before mama and daddy wake up. Besides, I'm keeping your plate theft a secret. You know she doesn't let us open up the holiday plates until it's party time."

"Ugh. Make me sick. Ugly self. Put some grits on my plate and bacon too, lots of bacon." I scoffed. "Don't play."

Donovan chuckled again. He was unbothered by my comment. This was what we did. We were some grown behind kids.

I walked out of the kitchen and into the hallway towards the front door. I cracked it open without peeping through the side windows. As soon as there was enough space to see who was waiting on the other side, I understood Donovan's laughter and hated I fell for his trap.

"Good morning, Harper." A covered dish was gently shoved in my direction.

"Oh, wow. Hey, Jabari. So good to see you. Hello, Kwesi. Nice seeing you again." I wanted to snatch the satin scarf from my head and at the very least run upstairs to wash my face and brush my teeth.

I could see the questions on Kwesi's face. He pointed in my direction as it registered where he knew me from. "The lady I picked up at the airport yesterday, right?"

I understood his confusion. I looked rough at the airport too, but this was another level of wrong. I reached up and slid off my scarf, revealing my low cut, and smiled.

"Yes, that's me. Sorry I look so scary. I just woke up not too long ago. I was in the kitchen so I ran over to get the door."

"My apologies, we didn't mean to wake you all. I wanted to drop this by to your mom. She invited us for dinner later and I wanted to bring this over before we went to run some errands."

"Wait — *what*? She invited you over?" I stammered.

He pointed over his shoulder. "Yeah, I live across the street over there in the red, brick house." He pointed toward a red brick, ranch style home. "We moved in last week. Your mom saw me unpacking and told me if we didn't have any plans, we were welcome to come over for the holidays. Is that cool with you?"

I shrugged. "This isn't my house. So if my mother invited the three of you over for dinner, then it is what it is."

Kwesi looked up at his father. "It will just be the two of us. Dad, I'm gonna go grab the car and pull up to get you."

I noticed the shift in their demeanor, but wasn't sure what I might have said to cause it.

"Did I say something wrong?"

Jabari's head dropped. He diverted his dark eyes away from me, while placing his hands in his pockets. "No, it's okay. Terri decided she no longer wanted to be a wife and left me—she left us. Hence my move. Last I heard, she's been running around town with some big shot. It's been about a little over three months now. I had been staying in a hotel up until now. Kwesi stays in the dorm."

"Oh—oh, I didn't know. I'm sorry, Jabari." I reached out to touch his shoulder.

"It's fine. She claims she's open to go to counseling and work things out," he muttered. "We'll see what happens. Listen, tell your mom thanks. We'll talk." Jabari walked away.

As I stood in the doorway, Donovan came up behind me. I looked over my shoulder at him.

"Dang, that wasn't as funny as I hoped it would be."

I sneered at him. "Of course it wasn't funny. In fact, it was kind of heartbreaking. You could tell they were both upset."

I always thought if Jabari felt the pain he'd caused me in high school, I would be vindicated. Instead, I wanted to be a friend and comfort him. As I watched them pull off, my mind raced on what made Terri throw it all away—I mean, she worked so hard to have him.

"Look out, Charles. Big Sis has another present to unwrap this Christmas."

I rolled my eyes. "Shut up, Donovan. Ain't nobody thinking about him in that way, and I'm not trying to get caught up in their drama. I have love and Charles is all I need."

"Say what? Let's back up. Did I hear you say that you...*you* ...are trying to avoid drama?

"You know what, how about you just go warm up my plate?"

"Yeah okay, but if you really learned anything from putting your two cents where it's worth nothing— you'll mind your business. 'Cause I can tell you want to know what happened, which will lead to you getting involved."

My lips twisted. "Like I said, I don't want any parts of that. Come on. Let's go see if you know how to cook."

He shook his head and walked toward the kitchen. As I followed, I couldn't help but look over my shoulder across the street at Jabari's home. If they were planning to come over for Christmas, it would only be a matter of time before Terri showed up, too. While I no longer needed closure, I also didn't want to reopen my ex files. No, I wasn't going to get involved. Besides, I had enough going on in my life and sorting through Jabari's dirty laundry was not on my to-do list.

# Chapter 5

Donovan passed me a plate, and fixed one for himself before he leaned against the island. We chewed in silence for a few, but my nosey behind couldn't stand it anymore. I had to find out what he knew. Not that I cared to get back with Jabari, but I had to know why Terri left. I wouldn't dare ask Jabari any questions about his relationship in front of my family. I had learned my lesson on blowing up spots—or at least I was trying to learn.

"How long have you known about Jabari and Terri splitting? My mind is officially blown. She worked so hard to get him and then to just one day decide, 'Nah I'm over this.' I mean whoa, who does that? Granted I don't know both sides of the story, but geesh. Talk about cold blooded."

I picked up a piece of bacon and took a bite. Donovan stirred his grits, a huge smirk on his face.

"What, Donnie?" I looked down at my clothes and touched my unkempt hair with my free hand.

"Don't you get tired of being in everyone else's business?"

"What? If I really wanted to be nosey, I would've asked him directly."

Donovan gave me a disappointed look and wagged his finger at me.. "I would think by now you would realize nothing good comes from your interference."

I inhaled. I'd hoped he had decided to leave the past with the wrapping paper tossed out from last Christmas, but it was apparent he was shifting the conversation to what happened between us.

"Bro, I'm sorry. I've never stopped being sorry about Paula, but she lied to you and it would have been wrong of me not to tell you Olivia wasn't your daughter."

His jaw clenched. Donovan pushed himself up and folded his arms across his chest.

"That's the thing, Harper. I knew she wasn't my biological child. I wasn't an idiot, but I loved Paula and that was what mattered to me." A beat and then, "I didn't feel the need to call her out, but you—you couldn't let me handle my affairs."

My eyes bugged. I had no clue he knew about Paula cheating on him. I found out because Paula sent me a text on accident while trying to text the real father whose name must have started with the same initial as mine. Or maybe she had texted us both around the same time. Either way, Paula's message was clear—she wanted Olivia's biological father to back off and she wanted Donovan to remain the only person Olivia knew to be her father. When I confronted her, she told him everything in a letter and fled to live with her family in Alabama.

I placed my hand over my heart. I couldn't believe what I just heard. Who knew my brother was so caring?

"Donnie, that's *huge* you loved her so much you were willing to accept her—flaws and all. Wow."

He chuckled, but the tone was bitter. "If you say you love a person and dismiss them without even trying to see if you both can come out of the storm stronger, then you may need to ask yourself if you ever really loved them. I love her. Not loved – love her."

I shook my head. All this time, I thought he was upset because his dirty laundry was aired in front of our entire family. He had been waiting on Paula to show up, but she sent the letter through one of their mutual friends. I had never heard Donovan talk about a woman the way he spoke about her. It made sense now why he hadn't really gotten serious with anyone else. He was still hung up on Paula.

I wanted so bad to find her and reconnect them, but I wanted to have a meddle-free Christmas and a chance to make things right with my siblings. Maybe if I could figure out what was going on with her, or talk to my brother and make him want to find her on his own.

"You love this, don't you?" He sneered.

"Huh? Why would I want you to hurt? Be serious," I stomped my foot. He couldn't honestly think I was happy he was without the one he loved.

He shook his head. "I'm not talking about me. I'm talking about what's going on with Jabari and Terri's relationship."

I tilted my head. "Again, why would I enjoy his suffering? I loved him back then and more importantly, we were friends over everything else." I looked toward the window, and back at Donovan. "I see she's still selfish as ever. Let me stop. That's not my business."

He nodded. "Sad to speak on it, but you're right about Terri. She's always been self-absorbed, and made herself a top priority over any and every one. They ain't even divorced yet, but she out clubbing and running behind some dude. She's as trifling as they come."

My brows rose as I closed the gap between us, thirsty for every drop of information on what went wrong with Jabari and Terri. "What happened, Donnie?"

He shooed me away. "Nah. You need to go talk to him – your *friend* before everything. I ain't about to sit over here and gossip like some teenage girls."

"Donovan—I'm not playing with you. Spill it. What happened with Jabari?"

"Well, well. Look who got up early to be messy instead of waking the rest of us up for breakfast," Wesleigh quipped. "Take down some plates from the pantry, Donnie. And Harper, stop being up in that man's business when you really need to be worried about Charles. Where is *he* for the holidays?"

I rolled my eyes. "He's in Aspen with the partners of his firm and their families. They usually go there every Christmas, which you know already because I told you this—*last* Christmas.

Wesleigh slopped grits onto her plate followed by a scoop of scrambled eggs. She grabbed a few pieces of bacon as well, and walked over to the kitchen nook to have a seat.

"Donnie, please make a sister a pancake, and Harper, I thought you'd finally given Charles his walking papers." Whipping her head back towards our brother, she said, "Oops, that's Donnie who breaks it off before the holidays...*my bad*."

Donovan eyed her from the stove. "Never piss off the person preparing your food, Sis. Remember that. Unless you ordered the special."

Wesleigh shrugged. "You act like it's a lie or something. Perhaps I should've asked first. So is *Eva* coming over for dinner?"

Donovan cleared his throat. Eva was the new girl he had been seeing. Since Paula, it had been a new face almost bi-monthly. They never stuck. Eva was more of an occasional hookup and not on the level I now knew Paula had been to him. Eva was fine with her status with Donovan. She was also a serial dater. Their agreement was odd to us, but they made it work for them. Now that I knew he couldn't get Paula out of his system, it made sense why he hadn't connected to anyone else.

"Go 'head on, Wessy, before I hurl this pancake at your face."

"As long as it reaches my plate, that's fine," she said with a triumphant smile.

I shook my head. "Wessy, I sure hope Santa brings you a new attitude or at the very least an understudy who can fill in for you over the next few days."

"Harper Layne, you ain't right. We don't wish away family. Not even as a joke," my mother scolded. "You're the oldest—act like it some time."

Every single time. She never wanted to come into the room when they were acting up. My mother's timing was always set to Harper Happenings or something. She only caught me when I attempted to get someone together for coming at me sideways.

"Good morning, Mother," I mumbled, turning to face her. "Perfect timing as usual."

My mother waved me away. "Was that Jabari I heard a moment ago?"

I rolled my eyes. "Ma, so you're telling me you heard Jabari's voice from upstairs, but you ain't hear Wessy getting slick at the mouth? Come on now."

My mother walked over to prepare her plate and ignored my query. That's what I thought. Selective listening at its finest. Only my mother. When we were in high school, my sister snuck out of the house at least once or twice a weekend, or snuck in if she missed her curfew. On one occasion, I had covered for her when my parents noticed she was late for curfew and made up some excuse for why she hadn't made it back yet, only for her to try to sneak back in stumbling all the way down the hall with a puke-stained halter-top. Instead of her getting in trouble, the burden was all mine to carry.

Not to mention my brother has had more pregnancy scares than I care to think about, but since I drove him and his girl of the moment to the clinic, again, I didn't do the right thing. I was supposed to set the example and fuss at them as if I were their parent, or at least that's how it always felt when my mother chastised me behind engaging in the foolishness with my siblings.

"So that *was* him. Did he drop off his dish? I wasn't expecting him until closer to dinner time."

"Yeah, Ma. He dropped it off not too long ago," Donovan chimed in when he saw my tight-lipped expression.

"And he moved over here when? That's new information no one thought to share?"

My mother sat down at the table and shrugged. "You have Charles now. I didn't think you'd care. Besides, it's sad what happened. That girl said she needed space and asked him to leave since they were living in her mother's old house. Can you believe it? I bet he wishes he had stayed with you, huh Harper?"

This was my cue to leave. My mother loved Charles, but she was a fan of romance novels and always wanted a fairy-tale ending where I ended up with my high school sweetheart.

"Welp, I'm gonna go shower and get dressed so I can run out to get *more* paper plates and *more* aluminum foil for tonight." I cocked my head to the side. "Is there anything else?"

My mother raised a brow and shook her head. "No I think that's all, Ms. Sass-a-fras."

I darted upstairs before I could show my mother just how sassy I was feeling this morning. Some fresh air would do me some good. I couldn't get upstairs to shower and change fast enough.

# Chapter 6

I pulled my Nissan Altima onto Powder Springs Road, and made my way to the Publix on Macland Road which was only minutes away from my parents' house. I considered vanishing and hitting up the mall, but I knew my mother would be calling about the foil since that's what I said I was going out for in the first place.

I turned the radio up as KISS 104.1 began to play "What Do the Lonely Do at Christmas?" by the Emotions. I always loved this song. Yes, it was sad, but they were so soulful I managed to look beyond the tragedy of the story of those who are left alone for the holidays. Granted, this was my current situation with Charles being away, but it was also by choice I wasn't with him. His firm had their traditions, and my family and I had ours.

I wasn't ready to make a commitment to give up my family once a year for him and his firm. If my time away from my immediate family meant I was celebrating with him and his family, that would be one thing, but being around his colleagues from the law firm felt more like networking than family bonding.

As I swayed to the music, my work cell rang.

"Harper Hilson of Hilson and Swain Realty speaking."

"Now that's what I'm talking about," the male voice said. "This is Felix, from the airport. How are you?"

I hoped he was calling with a referral already because that would make the perfect Christmas present—commission never needed a bow.

"Yes. Good to hear from you. I hope all is well."

Felix chuckled. "Couldn't be better. So after doing a quick search on the Internet, you seem to be highly recommended. I'm for sure going to refer you to some of the rookies I sign and anyone in the league looking for a house. At the moment, I'm the one who could use your assistance."

I reached up and brushed my shoulder off—we did work. We tried to be a one-stop-to-closing business, and we were blessed to have accomplished our mission with the vast majority of our clients.

"Okay. I recall your fiancé saying you all lost the house you were looking to purchase. How soon are you looking to move?"

"To be honest..." He laughed nervously. "We've been renting and didn't renew, and the owner notified us today that they've already leased the place. He's giving us two months to secure another place to stay."

"Wow, what a way to start the holiday. How terrible."

He cleared his throat. "Are you free today? I know it's Christmas Eve, and very last minute, so I do understand if you can't accommodate me today."

My eyes bucked. I guess my mother would be cursing me after all, but I planned to drop off the foil and make a quick run. It was still early in the day. I checked the clock on the console, and it was after ten in the morning.

"I can make it happen. If you can, send me a text or email with a budget and a few must have amenities. This information will assist me in pulling properties I feel are worth your time. Once I have that, just give me an hour or so to check and see which properties are available to view today. Would that work?"

"Sounds perfect. See you soon."

We disconnected the call and I sent Keesa a quick message to let her know we were in business. Between the two of us, we could have him locked into a home before the day was over. This year had been really good to us, and I had a feeling showing this property today was going to open up more avenues for our business to grow. *NFL— we are open to your business*, I thought with dollar signs in my eyes.

# Chapter 7

After speaking with Felix on the phone, I arranged for us to see a few properties near Flowery Branch, where the Atlanta Falcons trained. Several of the Falcons lived close to the training facility and preferred to find homes in Gwinnett County during the season. I was fortunate enough to have three properties available to view today, and I really felt he would choose one of them to be his new residence.

The first property I asked him to view had three bedrooms and two and a half bathrooms, and a double-car garage. I was certain he would fall in love with this property once he saw the relaxing and romantic view of Lake Oconee from the upper balcony off the master bedroom. I pulled up to the brick, three-story, luxury townhome, and walked inside to do a quick review of the home. Satisfied that everything was on point, I went downstairs and placed some brochures and business cards on the counter.

Within minutes, there was a knock.

"Hey, Felix. Come on in."

"Thank you. If the interior looks as good as the exterior, then I'm hyped for what you have in store for me today."

I grinned. "Excellent. I have some quality homes in store for you today, but I started with the one I think might be your frontrunner."

As he walked through the entryway, I inhaled his cologne. Versace Eros. I knew that scent well. I bought it for Charles when we first started dating, and he'd been wearing it ever since. God, I missed him. He would really love this property. He was a true Georgia boy and loved to go fishing. During the day he was all suits, but when he actually took a minute to enjoy life, he was flannel shirts, tackle box in hand and—

"Harper, did you hear me?" Felix interrupted my thoughts.

"Oh, I'm sorry. No, I didn't actually."

He raised his brows. "No problem. By the smile on your face, that must have been one heck of a daydream." He patted me on the shoulder. "Let's see the rest of this house."

I could feel my face turning red. I nodded and gestured for him to step ahead.

I gave him a thorough tour of the house. When we were done, I led him into the kitchen. "I understand you love to cook, but I'm willing to bet you'll love it even more overlooking Lake Oconee." I raised the blinds so he could see the view.

I had left them down on purpose because I wanted a dramatic reveal.

His eyes widened and he put his hands on top of his head. He was in awe and I was in heaven. *Mission accomplished.*

I opened the door leading to the backyard, allowing him to get a better view of the well-manicured lawn and amenities the property had to offer. I was certain he would love the built-in grill on the patio, ample seating for entertaining, and the fire pit set up beyond the deck.

He walked out into the yard and turned around, taking in the landscape. "I can see the vision for this. I've always wanted a yard this size. I can see family get-togethers and of course football season is going to be on-point out here."

I stood back and watched him marvel. This was what I liked to see. When clients started to visualize, you let them and never disturbed their state of awe and imagination. This helped us sell houses.

I spoke again, drawing him back to me. "Are you ready to see the master bedroom?"

He turned and looked at me showing every single tooth in his mouth. "Man, I'm in sensory overload but yeah, let's do it."

Just as he approached the deck, his cell phone rang. He looked up at me, his eyes still filled with wonder.

"Hey, umm… this is my lady friend. She's out front now. Is it cool if we grab her before we look at the bedrooms?"

"Of course. Why don't you hang out and I'll go let her inside?"

He nodded and I left him outside overlooking the lake to envision the cookouts and family gatherings he would have in the future.

I checked my watch. It was almost noon. I hoped Felix's fiancé loved the place as much as he did, and they wouldn't even want to bother looking at the other spots. That would allow me to get this deal going and get back to help my family with the rest of the day. I hadn't checked my phone yet, but I was sure there would be a message from my mother waiting.

I unlocked the door and opened it, but the woman waiting on the other side wasn't the woman I expected to see. She had her head turned, no doubt still on the phone with Felix.

"Excuse me, hello I'm Harper. I told Felix I would escort you—" I opened and closed mouth. I was befuddled. My eyes had to be deceiving me. I found my voice and managed to mutter, "Terri?"

Terri Fordham. My old nemesis, the girl who stole my high school sweetheart—HER. Standing at the door, tapping her foot like I was the unexpected guest. Today was just becoming more eventful than I would like—and not in a good way. First Jabari, now Terri. What was really going on?

"What are you doing here?" we said in unison.

My eyes widened. "I'm his realtor." I looked over her shoulder expecting to see his fiancé, Meeghan. "How do you know Felix?"

Terri crossed her arms over her chest and took a step closer to me. I was slow to make the connection, but once the pieces came together—my mouth flew open. Felix must be the big shot Terri was gallivanting around town with.

I pulled the door up behind me and looked around to ensure Felix wasn't coming around the side.

"Listen, Terri, I don't know what's going on here, but I do know you're married to Jabari. Maybe you should go before things get messy."

She shook her head. "No, you *listen.*" She poked me in the chest. "I know what you're thinking, but what you *should* be thinking is how I can help you sell this house."

I chuckled. "If you know like I know, I wouldn't be so ready to buck over someone like Felix."

I knew I probably shouldn't have said that, but she needed to know she wasn't the Bachelorette and there would not be a rose ceremony in her future.

She stepped closer to me. "I don't know what you mean, but hear me when I say he'll listen to me. It sounds like he already loves this house, but I don't have a problem with convincing him otherwise. I don't want to wreck this deal for you—by being nitpicky. Know what I mean?"

I ignored her attempt at cutting a deal to keep her secret relationship with Felix between us girls, and went back to doing my job. I stepped back to allow her in.

"I'm letting you in because he's invited you here, but I don't want no parts of whatever y'all two have going on. This would kill Jabari. I thought y'all were supposed to be working it out, or at least that's what I heard."

As she coolly strolled by me, she looked over her shoulder and spat, "Why don't you leave my husband to me? I got him, remember? I clipped the claws you had in him a *loooong* time ago. How about you mind your raggedy business and work on helping Felix close on this house."

She clapped her hands together. "Chop, chop, Harper…we've got a house to see."

I gritted my teeth. Boy, this day was full of surprises – first Jabari and now this. If I had Jabari's number I would—no, no I would not call him. This was none of my concern. My priority was getting this money and staying as far away from their drama as possible.

But then again, Jabari and I used to be friends and I would want to know if my spouse was cheating on me. Furthermore, if my spouse was looking to purchase a home to shack up with his side piece, I'd want to know. Then again, my silence could lead to a meeting with killer karma—and I was not trying to see that heifer.

*Shake it off, Harper.* I had to keep in mind this was just business, and their affairs had nothing to do with me.

Once outside, I watched as Terri raced over to Felix and jumped into his arms. Similar to the way Meeghan had done at the airport the other day. I saw her whispering in his ear and turned away.

"I'll take it," Felix called out to me.

"Huh?" I exclaimed. "Without seeing the rest of the house?"

Keesa would have swatted me for the last comment, but I was surprised. Or at least I was until I saw Terri grin. A hush agreement. Oh goodness, she was trying to keep me quiet with a sale. She was a slick little something. Typical Terri, trying to get her way by any means necessary.

"Where and when do we sign?" Terri asked.

I held up my finger. "Let me just make a call."

There was a clear conflict of interest here. I would have to call Keesa on this. I knew she'd help me get back focused on the task at hand, which was business. As a matter of fact, I needed to have Keesa handle the rest of this deal.

I hadn't spoken to Jabari in years, but with him living across the street from my parents, if I got involved, it would be another Christmas filled with tension. I could see it now. My siblings confronting Jabari, and ridiculing me for not telling him. I was in a true Catch 22… and I was so confused on what I should or shouldn't do to get out of this hornet's nest.

I looked back over at the adulterous lovebirds. Terri smiled and winked at me before planting a deep kiss on Felix's lips.

He looked over at me with a guilt in his eyes. I shook my head—Keesa was going to love this.

# Chapter 8

Keesa picked up on the first ring. "So how is it going with the Worthington property?"

I could hear the excitement in her voice. Her eagerness reminded me this wasn't just my business and I had to remove the personal.

I ran my fingers through my hair and started rubbing the back of my neck. "It's going great," I replied, sheepishly. "He wants the place and is willing to pay full asking price."

I could hear Keesa clap her hands together. "Awesome. I knew he would love that place. You made a great selection. Do you have your tablet? I can start the paperwork and send it over so they can e-sign."

I sighed. "You know I do."

"My girl. Go ahead and get going and send me an email with some details so I can do some things on my end. It's time to pop some bottles tonight. Looks like I'll be coming over for your family's Christmas dinner after all."

"Good. We'd love to have you," I responded, my tone lackluster.

"Um—am I missing something? We just made some money with a new client who will recommend us to his clients. What's up?"

I looked over my shoulder at the couple exploring the house. "Well...you remember my high school sweetheart and the girl that stole him away?"

"Jabari and Terri, right?"

"Yep. My day started with finding out Jabari now lives across the street from my parents, and she's invited them over to eat. Jabari and Terri got married, are separated, and now Terri's here with Felix—not the fiancé he was with earlier at the airport."

"*Dang.* That's awkward, but it's not our business, Harper. He's a client – not your best friend or family. Besides, you said you haven't spoken to Jabari in years. Who cares what they have going on? Stay out of it."

I nodded as if Keesa could see me. "Yeah, I guess I'm feeling conflicted because we have history. And I'm scared when I see him at my parents' house that I'll tell it all."

"No, you won't because I'll be there to have your back." Keesa huffed. "What do you want to do?"

"This is *our* business, not solely my business, so I'll move forward with this as I would any other transaction. More than likely, I won't see Felix again anyway after this and I doubt I'll run into Terri. Up until today, we hadn't crossed paths. Or maybe Felix and Meeghan have an open relationship, and I'm a clueless outsider."

"You never know. All we know right now is there's money on the table and we have bills to pay."

I laughed. I knew Keesa would put things into perspective. "Okay, let me go handle business."

My conscience gnawed at me, but I didn't want to comprise this opportunity based on my eyes alone with no facts. Well—outside of Meeghan having that rock on her hand and Jabari saying Terri had been gallivanting around town with some guy—I didn't know anything concrete.

Yeah, right. I wasn't even convincing to myself. There was no way I was going to be able to hold this secret. I had to figure out a way to help Jabari.

But in the meantime, I would take care of business. I told Keesa I would, so now I had to do my part to close this deal. I opened my bag and grabbed the paperwork, and met the couple back in the kitchen. I raised my pen and said, "Shall we begin?"

An hour later, I was pulling back into the driveway at my mother's house. It was going on two in the afternoon, and I could only hope she wasn't about to chew my head off. I had enough on my mind as is – not that she knew or would care – but I didn't need another stressor.

I got out of the car and grabbed two bags of groceries from the trunk. I had stopped and got some champagne, fruit, and more paper plates and aluminum foil. We went through all of that quickly, so I thought it would get me some brownie points to buy more for the festivities.

"Hey y'all." I walked into the kitchen. Seemed like we were always in the kitchen.

"Hey," they all said in unison. It was my mother, sister, and Aunt Ephranette.

The sounds of Christmas blared through the radio sitting on the counter. My mom hummed along with the Temptations wishing everyone a Merry Christmas while she was shucking peas. My sister was peeling sweet potatoes for the candied yams and her famous sweet potato pies. And Aunt Ephranette was bumping her gums gossiping about whomever. I walked over to the pantry and pulled out packaged, seasoned, bread stuffing mix, and over to the refrigerator to remove a stalk of celery and one small onion to make my stuffing.

My mother looked up from her bowl, one eyebrow raised. "Did you make a deal? I hope so, since this big shot was asking you to show him something on Christmas Eve."

"Oh, I sold the house, and I made a deal ... with the devil. You'll never believe what happened. I was there meeting this guy to show him the house, and then guess who showed up?"

Wesleigh jerked her head in my direction. "Holdup...so now you're about to gossip about strangers?"

"Actually, you know some of the people involved." I snickered awkwardly. "I mean really this whole thing is a mess. What I could tell you would blow your mind."

My head cocked to the side as I smiled, waiting for Wesleigh or anyone to ask for more details, but they never did.

My mother nodded. "Hmm, well I'm glad you sold the house. That's a great way to start off the holiday with a little Christmas donation." She winked at me. "Now make sure you keep your nose out of other people's business so you can keep the sale."

I took that as my prompt to continue getting my ingredients from the pantry and cabinets to make my stuffing. I could hear the television from the garage. My dad and brother were outside either about to deep fry the best turkeys ever or have us appearing on the evening news. Last year, they almost burned the house down, not paying attention to the turkey. We compromised this year and told them to take a television outside to watch some games while they cooked.

"Wessy, is your friend still coming over for dinner tonight?" mom asked.

Wesleigh huffed and looked in my direction. I guess she didn't want me in her business, but if this mystery person was coming over, I would have to meet him eventually.

"Yes, I have someone who might stop by, but I doubt they'll stay for dinner. She's got her man with her. I hope that's okay."

My mother pursed her lips. "I can't recall the last time you brought a man around. All you do is work. Do you ever take the time to even try to date?"

I swallowed hard and continued to focus on my dish. I knew what was coming next. I could feel my sister's eyes boring into my soul.

"I wouldn't have to grind as hard as I am, if *Harper* would've minded her own business when I had the chance of a lifetime."

Wesleigh was approached by an entrepreneur who wanted to publish a sports and fitness magazine. He'd offered her a position covering stories on fitness and nutrition. At the time, she was an aspiring fitness model and worked full-time as personal trainer at a local gym. Wesleigh jumped at the opportunity to work with him. She believed this role with the magazine would put her in touch with fitness industry professionals, and making those contacts would benefit her once she got her well-being and fitness facility up and running. Everything appeared to be legit, until he wanted to take some photos of her in a barely there bikini and in suggestive poses that didn't look like anything I'd ever seen in a fitness magazine.

Needless to say, I interceded and got way too involved, asking for his references and a portfolio of photos he'd done before. Wesleigh was too focused on the best case scenario, so I had to do the due diligence for her and find out what he was hiding. I researched him to see if he was known and involved in the industry. By the time I was done grilling him, he pulled the offer.

He said he wanted to work with someone who was mature enough to handle her own affairs, and felt like my constant interjections would prove to be a deterrent in the long run to the vision they had for the company. Wesleigh objected, but the damage had been done.

"Wessy, he seemed seedy." I fussed. "I was trying to help. There was no way of knowing *FitNecessary Magazine* would thrive at the level it has or be so well received in the industry."

Yes, I had been wrong, but I still thought the guy had crooked beginnings that ended up working out in his favor.

"True statement. You didn't know and I didn't know either, but I was taking a risk to see where the opportunity would take me and you killed it. I could've had more than one little rinky-dink workout studio by now."

I inhaled and shifted my eyes back to my stuffing. I'd apologized multiple times to her and my brother, but I guess I was asking for too much to have them forgive me. It had been a year, and things were decent between us, but I knew it was based on trying to make the holidays pleasant, and had nothing to do with forgiveness.

"But I don't understand how or why you think the magazine was your golden ticket to expand? You can still do that. I can help you find a space."

"The connections I could've made would help me have the income to do it bigger, better, and faster. It's taking me a while to save towards expansion, but imagine if I had celebrity clientele. That could've been huge, Harper."

I filled my cheeks with air and blew it out. "Wessy, again, I'm sorry. I overstepped. You're right. I should've let you handle your own affairs.

She nodded and I left it there. I would claim this as a truce, and enjoy the rest of the day with the family and keep it moving.

I poured my stuffing into the casserole dish, and placed it in the oven. As I glanced around the kitchen, it seemed most everything was done. I took that as my chance to dip out and get the papers finalized for the Worthington property before more people arrived.

As I climbed the stairs and walked into the bedroom to retrieve my laptop, I couldn't help but think about Terri's scandalous behind and Jabari. My siblings were right though. Every time I attempted to help someone, I got in the way and made a mess of things.

I was taking a backseat to all the drama being thrown in my direction, and I was staying focused on real estate and my own affairs. Like I told myself before getting off the plane, I was only going to offer help to those who asked for it. Everyone else would have to fend for themselves. Content with my decision, I turned on my laptop and got to work.

# Chapter 9

I wrapped up my Skype call with Keesa and sent Felix the e-link for the offer on the property. Once I got the signatures, I would send to the seller's agent. Keesa had sent over a preapproval letter to go along with the offer. Things were in motion and I still felt conflicted. Nonetheless, I had resisted the urge to go tell Jabari and so far no one in my family knew the details. I was proud of myself.

I exchanged my business attire for some Atlanta Falcons fan gear to join my family to watch the game. The home team would be playing in New Orleans tonight, so I had to go downstairs and represent with the family. That was one tradition that brought us together despite our differences.

As I reached the bottom of the stairs, I smiled as I heard everyone talking over each other and laughing loud—our native tongue. Outsiders always wondered why we yelled when we talked, and I could only describe it as the natural flow of conversation with our family. We joked and the only volume we knew was loud. It was so natural we didn't notice how extreme we were, until someone more soft spoken came around.

I walked over and plopped down on the sofa next to my dad who was shuffling a deck of cards. I knew that meant spades were on deck before the game. We were very competitive when it came to playing cards and bones. My father treated dominoes like an Olympic sport. He just knew he was wearing gold medals around his neck. I was right there with him. I was super competitive when it came to cards, board games, and dominoes. Bring it.

"Daddy, you ready to teach them how we do in spades already?" I joked. "Isn't it too early for us to hurt their feelings?"

"Nah, never too early for that," he said, turning to pound fists with me.

Donovan was the first to object. "Here y'all go. Unc and I give y'all a run for it every year."

"Running and crossing the finish line victorious are two different things, Little Brother. I been telling you for years I would train you to be a champ like me and Daddy."

"Girl, you talk more junk than your daddy," Uncle Lafayette retorted. "But you know good and well you can't back none of it up, young'un."

I tilted my head to the side and chuckled. "Let me see how fast that check you wrote will bounce. Let's do this, Daddy."

My brother hopped up from the floor and cleared the card table so we could prepare to throw down. My dad did a quick riffle shuffle style on the deck. I cut, and started passing out cards. This was our Christmas. Food, family, and talking loud.

After an hour of calling out bids, killing kings and queens, and reneging—by Uncle Lafayette—it was finally time to eat. This was the first of many plates. More of my family would be joining us later. Just as my father was about to say the prayer, I heard a knock at the front door. Wesleigh went to answer it and returned with Jabari and Kwesi.

They fell into the circle, joining hands with the person closest to them. I stole a peek at Jabari before bowing my head. He looked in my direction. His eyes looked swollen and tired. I closed my eyes as my father began praying.

As we all said amen, I looked up to see Jabari turning and heading straight to the living room. I followed.

"Hey, Jay. Not hungry?" I inquired.

"Yeah, I'm starving but considering that your family is large, I figured it wouldn't hurt to let your family go first and grab mine toward the end."

I nodded. I walked further into the room where he was standing. I chewed on my bottom lip, trying to keep my mouth busy doing anything other than talking. I wanted to tell him I was sorry for his marital problems, but I knew the best thing to do would be to talk about anything other than Terri.

"I'm really sorry about you and Terri."

As soon as the words left my mouth, I wanted to suck them back in. This was not the best time to pick at his wounds. He played off the ache I saw in his eyes.

"It is what it is. She's doing what Terri does best – look after Terri. How have you been?"

I took his cue to change the subject and obliged. I half shrugged. "I can't complain. The real estate business is going well for us. I'm actually made a sale this afternoon. So I'm good."

I secretly hoped he would inquire about the property I sold so I could drop some hints that would allow me to tell him about Terri. If he asked questions, then I wouldn't be snitching. It would've simply come out in conversation.

"Congrats," he said while in motion toward the bookshelf. "I saw a few of the billboards. You're doing your thing."

Awkward silence ensued. I scratched my head and fiddled my thumbs before turning to head back to the kitchen where it was safe. The silence was deafening. "Well, make yourself comfortable. I'm about to get in this line and grab a plate."

"Yo," he called out after me. "Is this the McEachern High yearbook from our senior year?"

"Yep, that's it. And I know what you're thinking. The design on the front is hot." I was on the yearbook staff, so my royal blue bind and silver lettering on the front looked as if I just got mine today.

He chuckled. "I should have known yours would be fresh from the plastic, bubble wrap crisp."

"Did you doubt? I'm still proud of this. One of our finer issues, if I can toot my own horn and I will." I lifted my arm up and down, pretending to pull a truck horn.

As he went to place it back on the shelf, a photo of us from Senior Day fell out. He stooped down to pick it up. As he stared at it, I took it from his hands and replaced it in the book. That photo captured so many memories. It was the very same day I found out my high school sweetheart was sharing his heart with someone else, and to pour more salt on my open wound, I found out he'd gotten her pregnant.

"If y'all are going to eat, you better come now. They aren't playing," Kwesi said from the door.

I was too happy to be saved by the plate preparation shuffle. "You don't have to tell me but once," I said turning toward the kitchen. "Come on Bari, let's go eat, drink, and be—"

"Merry," he said, his tone less festive.

"No silly, eat, drink, and be fat ass full."

That made him guffaw and I was happy for the distraction. His eyes held memories and questions of what if, or at least I assume that's what was linked to the sadness I saw. We were happy then, and now he was going through a strain in his marriage. Whether or not that was temporary for them, I didn't know and I wasn't going to dig for any details. Not today. Not tonight. No drama this Christmas. Not if I had anything to do with it.

I tugged on his hand and nodded toward the aroma of baked candied yams, brown sugar basted ham, and green bean casserole. The sweet smell of apples baking in my aunt's beloved apple crumble wafted from the oven to our noses as we made our way towards the rest of the family. My mouth watered, taking me away from Jabari's pain to focus on the task at hand—putting these stretch pants to good use.

# Chapter 10

Beyond stuffed, we all lay around the living room until my mother revived us from our food comas. Jabari and Kwesi hadn't too long left. I knew shopping with the Nettes was right around the corner.

"All right, y'all need to get a move on. We got some shopping to do," my mother announced, high-fiving her sister.

Groans and moans escaped us all. I willed my head to lift from the pillow that held me as its willing hostage. The last thing I wanted to do right now was shop, but it's what we did every year. Fat-A-Full or not, we got up and went to the Night Before Christmas sales, and tonight, our goal was to conquer Wal-Mart.

My mother and father were adamant about having a Smart television, and they had to have it on Christmas morning. So they were pushing us to get up before our food got the chance to properly digest.

I looked at my watched and turned toward my eager mother. "Mama, the sale doesn't start until eight o'clock. It's six. We have time." I rolled back over.

The symphony of grunts surrounding me were a clear indication that my siblings and my father were also not ready to get out in the holiday havoc.

"Oh no, you don't," Aunt Ephranette yelled. "Y'all get on up and let's get going. We got to man our aisles and get in formation like the song say. The routine ain't changed. Let's hit it."

An hour and several frustrated, grumbles later...we were in the Wal-Mart parking lot listening to our assignments for operation.

"Okay, Lafayette and Donovan, y'all go to electronics or wherever they're putting the televisions. That's the main purpose of our visit. Don't let me down," my mom commanded.

"Yes sir, Boss. Anything else, Boss Lady?" Uncle Lafayette joked.

My mother responded by rolling her eyes, and turning her attention towards me. "Harper and Wesleigh, you both go on over to housewares. One of y'all get the vacuum and the other get that new model Ninja—it's on sale," she barked, like a drill sergeant. "Ephranette and I will comb the center aisle and be available on walkie-talkies with backup carts in case a battle ensues."

My sister and I looked at each other, and turned toward the store. I could already tell this was about to be a mess. Even more so when my aunt yelled after us all.

"All right y'all. This ain't for the weary. Only the strong survive—don't punk out and don't be giving in to little old ladies trying to chump you for the goods. Leggo."

"Is she for real?" Wesleigh queried. "It's not that serious."

"You must not recall the incident where I had to talk the officer out of arresting her the last time we all went shopping."

Wesleigh stopped in place, her mouth agape. "Shut up. How did I miss that?"

"You were mad at me and got to work with Ma that year," I said, stopping to stand within earshot of her.

Taking a moment to recall the last time we all went shopping together, Wesleigh nodded and sighed. It wasn't a great moment for any of us. This was one of our traditions, and every memory had been a pleasant one— before last Christmas.

"Wesleigh, I won't interfere in your affairs anymore. I was wrong to do that. You're an adult and you know what's best for you."

Her face softened and her shoulders relaxed. "I know you were only trying to help. I'm madder at myself, in retrospect, for not being more vocal to let you know I had it under control. My studio is doing well, but I still think the opportunity could've given me more exposure."

"It'll happen if it's meant to happen, and you know that's a part of your destiny. It'll come and when it does, it'll be bigger than *FitNecesssary.*"

She nodded. "I still want to reach out to him and see if that window is even partially cracked for me to get a second chance."

"Maybe you should. Perhaps invite him over for family dinner tomorrow if he's free or day after Christmas." I leaned into her side. "Nothing to lose here. Take a chance."

"Y'all waiting on an Uber to get y'all to the entrance? My Lord," Aunt Ephranette complained, bolting past us.

"I can't wait to get this over with," Wesleigh whined.

"Let the battle for bargains begin."

One of the store attendants came over the loud speaker to announce some of the hidden sales happening around the store. Wesleigh and I got over to our designated section and separated. There was a cluster of men and women waiting to get the latest, which from the looks of it was the Dyson and Hoover brand vacuum cleaners.

The death glares I got as I entered the aisle just to take a look at the product specifications made me roll up my sleeves. I knew I would be calling for back up. I began to stretch my limbs and open and close my palms to stretch my fingers out. I needed to have Bruce Leroy grip messing with these folks today. I reached into my back pocket and sent Wesleigh a text that I might require some muscle as soon as she snatched up a Ninja.

My mom and auntie were so serious about this shopping business. Everyone was ordered to wear loose fitting pants with pockets that zipped so we could carry the essentials—keys, cards, and cell phones. My walkie was clipped to my waist. These shoppers were in for a battle if they thought I wasn't 'bout that life. I wasn't, but they didn't know that and auntie wasn't trying to hear it. If I didn't come out of the dust with a vacuum, there would be all levels of hell to pay.

"Harper, is that you?" a female voice said.

I turned around to see Paula, my brother's ex standing in front of me. She was with two other women who appeared to be in their early thirties as well.

"He—hey, Miss Lady," I replied. "How are you?"

"Doing well. Just out here trying to get a few deals." Her eyes bore into mine. "I may not be a part of the family anymore, but this was a tradition I continued. Hope you don't mind."

I held my hands up in defense. "Why would that bother me? This isn't something my family does."

She chuckled, but the tone showed she was uneasy. "I know. It was a joke." She glanced past my shoulder. "Is Donnie here, too?"

"Electronics. You know we got to have him over there to get the heavy stuff."

She looked away and back towards her friends. Against my better judgment, I opened my big mouth and regurgitated everything I'd felt since finding out Donovan's true feelings.

"Listen," I whispered. "I didn't know. When Donnie told me he didn't care the baby wasn't his and that his knowing had no bearing on his feelings for you, I felt so bad. I didn't realize he knew all along. I should've stayed out of it. I'm sorry."

The shocked expression on her face let me know she didn't know either and once again, I had inserted myself in Donovan's business.

"3-2-1...happy shopping everyone," the store clerk announced.

I stood still standing face to face with Paula for what felt like forever. Her face went from shocked to thoughtful, to angry. Her anger was reserved for me. She must not have known Donovan knew, and now that she did, she was probably even more pissed that I broke them up.

It wasn't intentional, but confronting her on Christmas last year had been in poor taste. Not checking to see if my family had come into the room to witness the whole ordeal was dumb on my part.

Hearing Auntie on my walkie-talkie brought me back to life.

"Chile, grab that vacuum and get your head out the snow. You're missing out on the good ones."

I shook my head and lunged into the hornet's nest of overly aggressive men and women, tugging, pulling, and pushing to get the top-of-the-line products. The screeching of sneakers against the tile floor along with the symphony of grunts were a welcomed distraction from the situation I'd created. I reached around two people fighting, snatched the vacuum they let slip during their scuffle, and darted toward the end of the aisle just in time to hear them yell after me. I hurled the box into Aunt Ephranette's awaiting cart and yelled, "RUN."

# Chapter 11

As Auntie and I got to the register, we began to unload our finds onto the counter. She cleared her throat and I knew she was about to talk about somebody or worse, say something slick towards me.

"Was that uh, Paula I saw you talking to when you should've been shopping?"

*Dang it.* Of all people, she was at the top of the list of people I would love to have not witnessed a thing. Not that she would run and tell Donovan, but she had a reckless mouth and the possibility of it slipping out in conversation was high.

"Yep, that was her."

I didn't offer any additional details. I wasn't planning to give away anything for free, but I would answer questions out of respect for her. I wasn't crazy and my lips were on lock down.

"Oh, all right. How she doing?"

I shrugged. "Looks like she's fine. We didn't chat long."

Aunt Ephranette stared me down. I was glad when the clerk finally provided a total so we could get back focused on our task and not my seeing Paula. I was happy to be getting out of here soon. Standing for an hour waiting for the sale to start and then another hour waiting to check out, I was good on shopping for the rest of the year.

As we pushed the cart outside, I was surprised and elated to see the rest of the family making their way out to the car as well. Good, we could head back to the house.

"How'd y'all make out?" my mom asked.

"I got everything on the list. We almost didn't get the vacuum 'cause Harper was distracted," Aunt Ephranette said.

My eyes bugged. I thought we'd at least make it to Christmas or New Year's before she would be careless, but here we were with everyone looking at me to see what had my attention. But God...but God had another plan.

Uncle Lafayette intervened. "Who cares? Y'all got what y'all needed—let's get moving. It's cold out'chere and I'm ready to eat some mo' of that ham."

"I know that's right," Donovan chimed in. "Come on, Unc. Let's load this car up so we can ride out. Y'all go ahead and hop in the car."

I glared at Aunt Ephranette as she sashayed toward the back of the SUV without a care in the world. Out the corner of my eye, I caught Wesleigh watching me, and wondered had she saw what happened. She was only an aisle over. It was possible.

As I turned in her direction, I knew she saw everything. Wesleigh shook her head in disappointment and walked over to open the car door. Just when she and I appeared to have come to a truce, she saw firsthand how I still managed to put my nose where it didn't belong.

The car ride back was quiet. I glanced over at Wesleigh, debating on whether or not to see what, if anything, she knew about my conversation with Paula. She was playing on her phone, or so I thought until my phone vibrated with a text message from her.

*Wesleigh: I saw Paula coming off the aisle you were on with tears in her eyes. I said hello, but she didn't speak back. Did you two talk? What did you do?*

The gall of her to think I said something. Yes, I may have tried to protect them when they could've protected themselves, but I didn't seek out drama by any means. I wasn't in the store hoping to run into Paula and my intent was only to apologize. How was I to know she never knew Donovan loved her daughter despite him not being the biological father?

*Harper: We greeted each other and I apologized for the hurt I brought to her and Donovan.*

*Wesleigh: ...oh that's all. That was a good thing you did. I guess she was overwhelmed to finally hear that?*

*Harper: I guess. Who knows?*

My response must have sufficed as she didn't send another text. I looked toward the front at Donovan and wondered if I should come clean. But then again, I'd omitted details from Wesleigh, and if she found out, then we'd be right back to where we were.

*Harper: Did you know Donovan knew Paula's kid was not his?*

Wesleigh inhaled and gave me a sidelong glance.

*Wesleigh: Nope. I'm guessing she didn't know either. Dang Harper.*

My shoulders slumped. I knew I'd stepped in it, and my shoes would not wipe clean easily. I sighed inwardly.

*Harper: When she approached me, I wanted to apologize and make good on everything. He told me, and I assumed he had told her. It was an innocent mistake.*

When Wesleigh reached across the seat and squeezed my hand, I was glad I had been up front with her—even after the fact. No need creating extra drama. Now I just had to let my brother know, which wasn't where I was finding the most difficulty. The tricky part was when and how to tell him, without creating another scene at Christmas.

# Chapter 12

I barely got any sleep that night, and it wasn't because I was waiting to see if my parents had stuffed our stockings and loaded our presents under the tree. Back in the day, my siblings and I would sacrifice sleep for the opportunity to tear at wrapping paper and play for a minute before crawling back into bed. No, that was not the case this time around. This time, I couldn't sleep because Donovan was on my brain.

A few hours before I finally went to lay my head down, Wesleigh and I stayed up talking over our cups of *adult* egg nog. I shared everything Donovan told me about him and Paula up to the Wal-Mart situation.

"I know it's going to be rough, but you have to tell him what happened. I know he'll be annoyed, but he handles you in his own way."

I nodded. "He's definitely more indirect in comparison to you. You like to put it out there, which is tough to receive, but I can appreciate it."

"Trust me. You want to let him know as soon as possible. What if she wants to call him and make amends?"

My shoulders lifted. "Then problem solved. She's the one that got away, and if she tells him she still loves him, then its goodbye to the rotating lineup, and hello Paula on the permanent."

Wesleigh pondered my words, taking a sip from her mug. "Or, he could be over it, and her calling could reopen a wound he doesn't want to pick at anymore."

"Well, there you go. He told me he still loved her."

Wesleigh tilted her head. "Just because he loves her doesn't mean he's ready to go back to that relationship. He might not be in love with her. There's levels to this thang."

I cringed. If Donovan had moved on like Wesleigh assumed, then Paula attempting to reconnect could prove more painful if he didn't have a heads up. It might not be a bad idea to let him know, but I had no way of knowing for sure how he would take it.

"Dang it, Wessy. The one time I try to right my wrong, I end up digging up more dirt."

She exhaled. "I say get out in front of it. If Paula pops up and mentions it before you, that could look like you're withholding information. Better you tell him before someone else does."

I nodded. Even now as I lay in bed, I nodded because I knew she was right. Depending on if Paula even resurfaced, how she presented what she found out could be the catalyst for more drama between me and my brother, or he might be thankful if it brought them back together.

I would much rather tell him than have the "what-ifs" dancing in my head. I swung my legs over the side of the bed and planted them on the floor. My body was prepared to take the long walk down the hall, but my head was sending out warnings that I shouldn't, or at least I should wait until after the family gathering. I decided on the latter.

I pushed up from the mattress, put on my favorite cozy, fuzzy socks and prepared to join everyone downstairs. I had a weird thing about my bare feet touching the floor if there was no carpeting. I grabbed my cell from the nightstand to see if I had any messages from Charles. Colorado was two hours behind, so we kept missing each other. Oh, how I missed that man. He sent me a picture of his legs resting on a ski lift.

*Charles: I don't want to take any more rides in this life alone. Care to join me?*

My heart swelled. If only he knew how much I wanted to be with him right now. If it meant I would have to sacrifice a family Christmas, I was seriously going to have to give it some thought. The more our love grew, the harder it was to be apart from him.

*Harper: Aww baby. I don't want you to have to go at it alone either—meaning that I would be there and not some snow bunny. Lol. I miss you more than you know.*

Walking into the family room, I was surprised to see I was the first one downstairs. Most of the time, it was

Donovan and I who started the party off. I walked across the hall and went into the kitchen to get breakfast started. I pulled out a carton of eggs and grabbed the bacon. After sitting it on the counter, I went to the pantry to get the grits. We normally ate lighter on Christmas morning. Just some basics and fruit—and mimosas.

I turned on the radio and started playing my mama's favorite Christmas mix that Donovan made for her. I was scrambling the eggs, humming along to "Santa Claus is a Black Man," when I looked out the window and saw Donovan and Paula talking in the driveway. *Crap.*

# Chapter 13

I began chewing on my thumbnail as I stared at them. From my vantage point, I couldn't tell if Donovan was happy, confused, or simply shocked to see Paula. I needed to get closer. Stop her from exposing our little secret. Or maybe she already had, and they were discussing how to dispose of my body. I rushed outside.

"Heeey. What y'all doing out here?"

I slipped my brother a curious glance, trying to gauge what he knew.

Donovan glared at me. "What do you want, Harper?"

"Nothing. Nothing. I was coming out to check the mail."

Donovan shook his head. "They don't run mail on Christmas."

"Oh yeah, that's right." I slapped my hand to my forehead. "I don't know where my mind was." I cleared my throat nervously.

We all stood there in silence. My eyes shuffled back and forth between Donovan and Paula. Their body language spoke volumes. Paula shifted between looking at her shoes, and Donovan's face. Donovan went from

Paula's face, to his shoes, and then randomly across the street.

"Uh, so Paula what brings you here?"

"After seeing you all out at the store last night—it brought back a lot of memories. I thought I'd come by and say hello. I didn't mean to intrude—I should go."

Donovan leered at me, before turning his eyes back to Paula. His eyes beamed as he took in the sight of her.

"It's good to see you," he managed to say. "How have you been?"

She exhaled. "It's good to be seen by you—and to see you, too. I'm doing well." She looked back down at her shoes.

He moved in closer to her, and I took a step back to give them some space. I knew I should leave, but I couldn't will my legs to move. I had to see how this was going to pan out. The way they locked eyes, it was like I wasn't even there anyway.

"And Livi? How is she doing?"

"Fine. She's gotten so big," she said, taking a step toward Donovan. "Listen, that's kind of why I'm here…"

I held up my hands to pause her. I wasn't sure what she was about to say, but I didn't want Donovan to blow up on me. Or take his frustration with me, out on her.

"Paula, I was just about to start breakfast. Did you want to come in and help me?"

"Um, we're kind of in the middle of a conversation here, Harper. Why don't you go back into the kitchen?"

I shrugged. "Eh, no rush. I can stand out here with you all. So Paula, what'd you buy at Wal-Mart?"

That was dumb, I thought. The last thing I needed to bring up was Wal-Mart, which is where I spilled the beans.

She huffed. "Harper, I'm sorry. I really need to talk to Donovan."

I waved her off. "That can wait. It's Christmas. It's time for food and adult egg nog. Come on, y'all."

"No, this can't wait anymore," Paula replied, ignoring my request. "Listen, I know you knew Olivia wasn't your daughter. Why didn't you tell me?"

"Whoa—what? How did—who—where did you hear that?" Donovan stammered.

I inched toward the door.

"Really, Harper? And you wonder why you're the last to know what's going on with this family? Just couldn't keep your big mouth shut."

"Does it matter if she told me?" Paula asked. She bit her bottom lip. "Look, I wanted to come over here and say thank you. You knew Olivia wasn't your child and yet you loved us both without limitations." She shook her head. "Who told you?"

This time it was Donovan who studied his hands and shuffled his feet. "I overheard you talking...on the

85

phone with one of your friends. You were telling her that…"

"I made a mistake." Paula wiped a lone tear from the corner of her eye. "It was the night after we had gotten into a huge argument about the prospect of marriage and we separated for a bit."

She stepped backward, putting some space in between them. I began wringing my hands together. This was such a mess.

"You didn't even want to marry me, Donovan. Why would you have accepted a child who wasn't yours? I know it's selfish, but I couldn't take the chance of you leaving me again—leaving *us*."

Donovan pushed his hands into his pockets, no doubt deep in thought. He had always loved her, but at the time he wasn't ready to take that last leap. Though we all knew they were headed in that direction.

"At the time, I wasn't ready to settle down. Actually, I was scared of the prospect of marriage. I didn't want to mess up what we had. But after our relationship hiatus, I realized how much I missed your company." A beat and then, "I wanted a family with you, and when you told me you were pregnant…I was so certain. I was sure Olivia was mine. It broke my heart to hear she wasn't mine."

Olivia had his eyes. His nose. The same cocoa skin tone and a matching cleft in her chin—all pieces of Donovan. He'd been there for her since childbirth. I took it just as hard as he did when we learned Olivia wasn't his seed.

"I can't apologize enough for hurting you. I was in a weird place, and there's no excuse for how I handled things. A lot has changed—and I would love a chance to tell you everything."

I could see Donovan struggling, and stepped up to take control. Yes I know, not minding my business, but what I saw was two people in love that couldn't figure out how to get back to happy.

"Would—would you and Olivia like to join the family for dinner tonight? I mean, I don't think we have any kid's gifts, but..."

The words flew out of my mouth faster than the thought formed in my head. Once again, I had inserted myself in my brother's business. The heat from his stare warmed the side of my face.

"We would love to—but only if Donnie is okay with us being here."

He nodded, but didn't say one word.

"So, it's settled." I threw up my hands. "We'll see you in a few hours?"

"Um, yeah thanks. We'll come by either before or after we leave my mother's house. Is it okay if I call you, Donovan...to figure out the best time to come over?"

"That's fine. Do you still have my number?"

She nodded. "I'll call you later."

He half smiled, and I exhaled. That went way better than I thought. I wasn't sure if this meant they were going to try to figure things out, but inviting her back into our family tradition was a start. I turned to head back into the house, but stopped short when I heard Donovan grunt. I didn't want to turn around to face him because I already knew he was going to be red hot and ready to beat my behind.

# Chapter 14

I raised my hands in defense. I knew he was about to tear into me, and to be honest, I deserved whatever was coming my way. Once again, I made an assumption which led to blowing up his spot—again.

"You enjoy the show, Harper?" he inquired, his arms crossed over his chest.

I chuckled for no reason. "Hey, listen, I happened to look up and see you two outside and—"

"You was scared Paula would tell me you been running your mouth again?" He chuckled. "So, let's hear it. What happened this time, Harp?"

I scrunched my nose and rolled my eyes.

"Okay, okay. Yes, I ran into her at Wal-Mart when we were all out shopping. I apologized about exposing her secret and told her I didn't know you knew about Olivia, and wished I could erase it all basically. But, as you know, she—didn't know your true feelings. I wanted to apologize."

He shook his head and walked over to me. I cringed because I wasn't sure if this was about to get ugly, or if he was about to hug me and put an end to our yearlong debacle.

When he stopped in front of me and kissed me on my forehead, I exhaled and leaned back to look at him.

"In some odd way, I feel like I should thank you because your meddling prompted her to come here and now she's coming over and bringing Olivia." A beat and then, "I really miss that little girl."

I smiled and he joined me. This was how it should've been, and I prayed this time they could make it work, and I could maintain my own lane and not interfere.

"That's a blessing, Donnie. I'm happy for you, and again, I'm sorry I managed to get wrapped in your business again."

"It was an accident—this time. No ill intent, and not that there was any last time. It just—things went wrong real quick. All is forgiven. Love you, Sis."

"Love you too, Donnie."

*Phew.* One family matter resolved, and one to go.

# Chapter 15

Heading back to the kitchen, I saw Wesleigh sitting at the kitchen table drinking a cup of coffee.

"Looks like things went well out there. Did you get to tell Donnie what happened in aisle six?" Her eyes smiled mischievously.

"No, she did not. Surprised you ain't come tell me something, Little Sis. What's up with that?" Donovan said, coming from behind me.

I shook my head. I didn't know why he was acting surprised that Wesleigh didn't snitch. She had always been the low-key sibling. She liked to stay to herself and kept her life free from drama—and private.

She twisted her lips. "When have you ever known me to be a stool pigeon? I told Harper to give you a heads up. I did my part."

I hastily responded. "And, *and*—I fully intended to do so, but as I got downstairs to start breakfast, you and Paula were already outside. It was too late to try to fix things."

He waved me off. "Like I said, we are good. The meddling actually served as an assist this time. But moving forward, when in doubt…shut your mouth." He winked at me and laughed.

I nodded. No words needed. The less I said, the better it was for everyone, apparently.

"So Wessy, your friend still coming by?" Donnie inquired. "And why aren't they visiting with their own people? Not many people travel to non-family members' houses during the holiday."

She rolled her eyes. "Everyone doesn't do holidays the way we do. She's from Cincinnati and wasn't traveling there this year. Anyway, not really our business. All you need to know is I expect you to be nice."

Donovan shrugged. "Aye, you know I don't even care like that. Just checking to see who was coming by later. Anyway, I need to go freshen up—since I low key got a date and all."

I watched as Donovan hopped up the stairs, taking them two at a time. He had a little more pep in his step. Talking to Paula seemed to agree with him.

I walked over to the table and pulled out a chair across from Wesleigh. "He looks happy."

Wesleigh nodded. She was scrolling through her phone checking messages. A frown formed on her face. I tried to resist the urge to ask what was wrong—tried, but failed.

"What's wrong with you? Your face went from relaxed to tense."

She looked up at me, one brow raised. I'm sure she was assessing whether or not to share what was going on with her.

"Nothing really. I saw Penny Anthony posted yet another monumental moment for *FitNecessary*. They landed Lailah Ali for the cover. Freaking Lailah Ali."

Penny Anthony was the trainer hired to take on the position at *FitNecessary* after I let it slip through Wesleigh's capable hands. Penny graced the first cover and if I was honest, the cover didn't come across as provocative as it had been presented. Or as I had assumed it would be. I'd messed up. Wesleigh would've have been living her dream working with top celebrities and athletes all across the country. Not that her business was performing poorly, but it wasn't at the height it could have been.

"Wesleigh, I can't apologize enough. I know that's probably not the right thing to say, but—"

"Harper, it's done. I'm just as tired of hearing you apologize as I am dwelling on the past. Besides, I have something in the works, and if everything goes as planned I'll be in a league of my own."

I remained silent and nodded. I was happy for her, but I'd keep my opinions to myself. Not that I had any on deck, but I was sure the more she spoke, it would only be a matter of time before I had a thought or two to share.

The sound of Wesleigh's phone vibrating broke the silence in the room. She put her attention back on her phone, and I got up to make myself a cup of coffee.

Looking over at Wesleigh as I added sugar and creamer to my cup, I could tell she was excited. Her eyes beamed as they had before, but this time, there was more confidence in her eyes. I felt comfortable knowing I didn't need to interfere. She had it under control.

"I'm about to go get dressed." I took a sip of my coffee and started toward the stairs. Looking over my shoulder, I said, "Good luck with your new endeavor, Wessy."

She smiled. "Thank you. I guess I better start getting ready, too."

My heart warmed. Turned out Christmas was going to be drama free after all. Donovan and Paula were reconnecting, and Wesleigh was tired of holding a grudge. I managed to stay out of Jabari's business without fail— everything was awesome. I hummed Christmas carols as I made my way to my bedroom looking forward to tonight.

The way the stars had aligned, nothing and no one would be able to disrupt our family tradition this year.

# Chapter 16

I pulled my dressing out the refrigerator and placed it in the oven to warm for dinner. The savory aroma of sage blended with celery, onion, and cornmeal escaped from the pan as I lifted the lid on the container. I inhaled and smiled. *I did that.*

I assisted my mother with getting the rest of the entrees and sides out. I could smell the fried turkey and my stomach began to curse me out.

The sight of my mother's giblet gravy percolating, and the thought of a plate piled high with gooey macaroni and cheese casserole, dressing, string beans, deviled eggs—I was having sensory overload.

"Harper, that dressing smells good, Hon." My mother's eyes beamed with pride.

"Why thank you, Mother. I learned from the best." She taught Wesleigh and I how to make her mother's prized dressing. It was a family recipe and we carried the torch well.

She began wiping down the counters and pulling out the plates and utensils. "I'm going to put this hen and the Honey Baked Ham in the oven later on."

I finished making the sweet tea and put it in the refrigerator to cool. A few minutes passed, and I noticed my mother was unusually silent. I cast my eyes over at her. That was not like her to work in the kitchen and not have any conversation or at least hum a little ditty. I could tell by the thoughtful look in my mother's eyes, she was thinking about something besides food.

"What's on your mind, Mama?"

She put the plates down and turned to face me. Her eyes glistened with unshed tears. Something was definitely bothering her.

"Are you and your siblings...okay? I know last year you had a falling out with both Donnie and Wesleigh, and I wanted to check to see if you all had smoothed things over."

I nodded my head. I was wondering when she would ask whether she should expect any foolishness tonight. And I didn't blame her for approaching me. It was my fault that last year's dinner had not one, but two incidents to disrupt our family dinner.

I nodded. "We're on the mend for sure. I've apologized to them both—several times—and we're working it out. I promise. I will *not* be the one bringing any drama this year."

Her brows drew together, and she folded her arms across her chest. "I'm sorry I put all of this on you, Sweetheart."

My eyebrow shot up. "Mama, what are you talking about? That was all me being too overprotective—"

"The way I raised you to be," she interjected. Her eyes welled up. "I instilled in you to be the protector. I made you do my job."

My nose crinkled. "What are you talking about? You're a wonderful mother."

"I thank you for that, Sweetheart. But when you were younger—at one point during the middle school or high school years—I tapped out. Your father retired, and then started his business, and I was just a mom—or *his* assistant. He was supposed to retire and then I was going to go back to school, but life didn't work out that way."

She shook her head. "You know, we got married and started our family at a young age—I was led by my heart and followed without a second thought of my future goals. I wanted to help Drew accomplish all of his dreams, then we started building our family and well, I forgot about me. You know?"

It still wasn't registering with me what she was trying to say. My mother was in every part of our lives. To hear her say there was a point where she felt like something was missing shook me a little.

I leaned against the kitchen counter. "What are you saying?"

"I placed a lot of responsibility on you to help keep your sister and brother in check. I had you in the mental space that it was on you to ensure they stayed out of trouble. I planted that seed in your head and for that—I apologize, Baby."

Sadness tore at my chest as she revealed her truth. My mother always seemed to have it all together and have all the answers. To hear she felt overwhelmed was new information I wasn't quite prepared to hear.

"Meanwhile, I was curled up reading books, going for walks, or taking my time in the store to avoid having to…be a mother." Her shoulders slumped as her bottom lip began to quiver.

I shook my head. "But you were a constant in our lives. I think you're being too hard on yourself." I reached out and took her hand. "I knew I wasn't the mother. It was clear who you were to us."

She chuckled, her tone solemn. "I guess, but you felt you needed to meddle and I planted that seed. Didn't just let you be a kid, you know? You were too busy trying to cover up for them or tell them what they should and shouldn't do."

"I suppose I can see where you're coming from, but I still had a childhood." I smirked. "Still managed to get into some trouble, too. You just never found out about it."

She swatted at me. "Well good, but still you know it's okay to trust your choices and enjoy life. Take some risks."

My face twisted in confusion. "What are you getting at, Mom? I do enjoy my life."

She dabbed at a tear threatening to escape. "Okay, okay. So what's going on with Charles?"

I could feel my cheeks redden. She always did have the knack for changing the subject. "We're doing well. He's good. Everything is cool."

She gave me a once over. "Never heard anyone describe their relationship as *cool*." Her sidelong stare was full of amusement at my expense. "Guess that's something the young folks say."

I chuckled. "Everything is fine. We're just at a crossroads is all," I admitted.

"Oh, I see. You're ready to be his partner for life, and he's ready to be a partner with his firm?" Wagging her finger, she said, "You tell him if he wants his future to include you, he better figure out a better way of showing it. That boy needs balance. You're not at his beck and call  he needs to get a clue."

I started to protest, but she wasn't lying. I didn't put the blame all on him though, I needed to speak up and tell Charles what I needed from him. If Charles could make me feel as important as he proclaimed, then maybe the notion of marriage wouldn't be so farfetched. And I was not willing to entertain that discussion with her or him until things changed.

Instead I nodded and said, "No worries there, Ma."

Appearing content, my mother dried off her hands and gave the kitchen preparations a last look. "I'm going to start getting ready for tonight. We have a little over an hour before people start arriving. Do you have this under control?"

"Yep. I'm pulling everything out and putting it in the warmer. Then I'll go get myself together."

She stopped on her way towards the stairs and kissed me on my cheek. "Make sure to call Charles and tell him we all said Merry Christmas and we wish he were here."

I smiled and watched as she disappeared up the stairs. I walked over to the sink, started washing the dishes and put them away. It never dawned on me I had taken on a parental role without being conscious of my behavior. I began to reflect on some of my maternal moments over my siblings, and her words started to make more sense to me. As I went deeper into my memory bank, there was a knock at the door.

I looked over at the clock on the microwave. It was too early for guests to arrive. I dried my hands and went over to answer the door. Waiting for me on the other side was the last person I expected to see today—or any day for that matter.

*Oh boy. So much for no drama.*

# Chapter 17

I made a mental note to fix my face before I opened the door. I knew me, and right now my eyes were bucked and lips twisted—nonverbal curses were on full display. It was one thing for her to pop up at the property with Felix, not knowing I was there, but she knew I would be here. *What could she possibly want?*

"Terri, hey—um—what are you doing here? I mean—well *uh*—Merry Christmas." I stumbled over my words.

"Yeah, Merry Christmas." A beat and then, "Hunh." She pushed a covered dish into my hands.

I looked down and held it up. "Thanks—what's this for?"

The stench that wafted from the container had me wanting to accidentally, on purpose, drop it. Yes, the glass would break and I would have to get her a new one, but it was a sacrifice I was willing to make to save my family from indigestion.

Crossing her arms over her chest, head tilted to the side, she said, "You did invite *my* family to dinner, *right*?"

"My mother invited *them* over…"

"*Them* equals me." She pushed past me to the hallway.

I stood there and took a moment. *No, this heifer didn't push me like I was nothing.* I took a deep breath, and waved away the evil thoughts I wanted to act out. "Come on in then," I mumbled.

Closing the door, I turned around to face the unnecessary, but necessary, standoff that should've occurred years ago. Terri's stare was menacing at best. It was apparent she had a lot she wanted to say—none of which I wanted to hear. I was sure she thought I was weak because I never stood up to her in high school, and hadn't even busted her out to Jabari.

I had to mentally prepare myself to not snatch her face off. *Remember what they taught you in Sunday school, Harper.* Though I tended to fall asleep during those lessons. Thoughts of asking for forgiveness flooded my head as I considered snatching her spine out.

We stood in the hallway. Her with her hands planted on her hips, and me stuck holding her ill-smelling contribution to dinner. Her right foot tapped the floor at a rapid rate. She thought her patience was wearing thin. I didn't appreciate this surprise drop-in or the unnecessary attitude. But I remained cool, as usual. I didn't let her see any emotion outside of nonchalance.

"Does this need to go to in the refrigerator?" I inquired. "What is it?"

"Chitterlin' casserole. It'll need to be warmed up."

*Or placed deep in the garbage—outside—in the neighbor's trash.* "Okay, cool. I'll put it in the fridge for now. The oven is full at the moment."

She shrugged. "It's whatever. So how you been?"

I'm not sure if it was the click-clack sound of her popping her gum, or the way she stood here with a high level of insolence—but I wasn't in the mood for any foolishness. I placed her dish in the fridge and continued in the unwanted banter she was attempting to have.

"Terri, you just saw me the other day. If you really cared about how I was doing, you would've asked me then. What do you really want?"

She crossed her arms over her chest and let out a harsh breath. "I bet it makes you happy, don't it? Knowing that Jabari and I are in a train-wreck of a relationship."

I inhaled. I would never wish any harm on him. She was a different story. I could care less what happened with her. As curious as I was about what really happened between them, Terri was the last person I wanted to talk to in order to get more details.

"All I know is you two are separated. The *why* is not my business," I said, walking toward the living room. I gestured for her to have a seat. "It's also not my business that your fast behind was jumping into another man's arms."

"Thank you for respecting our privacy. And thank you for being the bigger person. I know it must be hard to have heard Jabari and I stayed together. It must have killed you, hearing we had married and had a child, while you're still—single and childless."

I smirked. "Terri, you can't be serious. You want me to be upset because of something that happened in high school? I'm happy with my life. I have my own business. I'm dating someone very special to me. I'm good. You, on the other hand, need to quit stringing Jabari along and let him go if you're going to be so bold as to buy a home with someone else."

She nodded, but I could see she wasn't happy to hear I was straight. The defeat in her eyes should have been rewarding, but it was evident she hoped I had failed at love, too. Or perhaps she was being salty toward me for another reason, but I wasn't going to participate in her nonsense.

"Glad your life is so perfect. Of course it is, though. You had the perfect childhood. Above average grades. The girl that never had to work out. The flawless skin—of course your life is going well," she said, clearing her throat.

She was silent for a moment, looking me over. I shook my head and kept my peace. No telling what she was thinking.

"So—are you wearing *that* to dinner? I guess I overdressed, but then I always did one up you on the fashions, Harper."

I sneered. This heifer stayed trying me. I guess her faded Christmas sweater and worn leather skirt was dressed up.

"I was finishing up in the kitchen when you knocked. I'll be heading up to take a shower and get ready in a moment. Do you want to wait down here or did you want to run across the street to freshen up—at *your* place? Or perhaps you want to go to your new beau's place. Does he live close by?"

I knew I was being spiteful, but she had that coming. She wasn't living there with Jabari, and that was one piece of information I was glad I had to make her back down. I wasn't trying to make her feel any kind of way, but you have to fight petty with petty.

Terri's face went blank. I knew that would shut her up.

"You go ahead. I'll be fine right here." Terri leaned back against the sofa and folded her legs beneath her as if she lived there.

I placed the remote in front of her, and darted upstairs to get dressed. I wished I had told Charles to come here with me. I needed him to have my back, and help me stay out of trouble. I needed his loving embrace. I walked over to the nightstand and grabbed my phone. There was a message from Charles waiting for me.

*Charles: Merry Christmas baby. I wish you were here. Love you always.*

I read his words a few times before sending a response.

*Harper: Merry Christmas to you too. I miss you so much. I wish you were here today. Last Christmas, and the one before that. I need you with me. Talk with you soon. I love you.*

Tossing my phone on the bed, I plopped down and started to think about how crazy relationships could be. There was so much I wanted to say to Terri about what I saw the other day. I wanted to tell her    if she didn't tell Jabari, I would. I wanted to tell her she was setting herself up for heartache because Felix had someone, too.

I think if I had, maybe she'd confess or do some self-reflection. I really think I could help her come clean and maybe save their relationship. If that's what Jabari wanted. I'd have to give him a call. Of course, I would let him talk and then when he gave me a window—I would tell him what he should do about his treacherous wife.

\*\*\*

An hour later, I had showered, dressed, and made my way back down the stairs. I allowed my eyes to scan the room, taking in the decorations. You could tell we loved celebrating the holiday together. Outside of the bay window, I smiled when I saw the illuminated nativity scene my mother had on the front lawn accompanied by my father's reindeer he fought every year to have on display.

The inside of the home was a child's dream, full of red, gold, and green ornaments, faux snow around the sides and hanging off the tree. Snow-frosted Christmas garland hung atop  the curtains and along the fireplace in the family room. Tinsel and twinkling lights added an extra bit of sparkle—it had been this way since we were kids. Hearing the sounds of Boys II Men singing "Let It Snow" brightened my mood, but then seeing Terri and Jabari in separate corners of the room looking as if they were at a funeral and not a Christmas dinner—did not.

At least Kwesi was being distracted by a few of my younger cousins. I wasn't sure if he knew them from school or otherwise, but he seemed to be enjoying himself despite the fact that his parents were in an intense battle of the brood. I hoped they managed to maintain their silence and not disrupt our family Christmas with any of their mess. Lord knows we had enough drama last year, and though I didn't invite either of them here today, I would feel a sense of responsibility to fix things. Lord help.

I made a beeline straight to the naughty nog as we liked to call it. Donovan always managed to get the right combination of bourbon and nutmeg when he made the drink. It hit the spot, and gave me the kick I needed before I could turn around and deal with this drama looming in the background of my family's dinner. But in my defense, this time I didn't invite the mess to the party—my mother did.

I took another sip and caught Wesleigh's eye. She mouthed, "Oh my God."

I shook my head and bucked my eyes. Wesleigh had no idea how crazy this whole scenario was. I hoped they would keep their issues for after dinner—across the street—at Jabari's house.

I looked over at the stove and my mother and aunt had pulled everything out. I timed everything just right.

"Y'all what's in this Tupperware?" Aunt Ephranette asked. She eyed the dish and turned it side to side. I took a long, slow gulp of my eggnog and glanced over at Terri to see if she was planning to own her funky little dish.

Terri walked forward. "Oh, I thought I would bring something since you all were so kind to invite us. That's my chittlin' casserole."

Aunt Ephranette's nose scrunched. I thought I would spit out my drink, but I held it together. Auntie never let me down when her reads were directed at others.

"Well, ain't nobody invite you, Baby. We'll just put this back so you can have it when you think about taking a to-go plate."

Terri clicked her teeth and rolled her eyes before heading back to her seat. Over the tops of our glasses of eggnog, my siblings and I shared in a moment. The tears forming in the corner of my eyes were a dead giveaway that I was about to explode with laughter if I gave in to humiliating Terri.

My father, always someone's saving grace, called everyone together so he could bless the food.

"All right, all right—y'all stop," he said, though when he winked at me I knew he wanted to laugh, too. "Let's go ahead and bless this meal. Father God, thank You for this food we're about to receive. Thank You for family and fellowship, Lord. We ask that You bless the hands that prepared this meal and let it be the nourishment we need to fulfill our bodies and give us health and strength. In Jesus' name…"

"Amen," we all said together.

My father started carving off pieces of the fried turkey. The aroma of candied yams, dressing, baked ham, macaroni and cheese casserole, and collard greens were present in every corner of the kitchen. There were at least thirty people including my immediate and some extended family, and Jabari and his small family, trying to fix a plate.

My routine at family functions was to get my drink together first and claim a spot at the table. It was either that or mess around and end up at the kid's table or the floor. I didn't want either of those choices, so I settled for not being the first to dip the spoon into the dishes.

I looked up to see Terri helping Jabari get some turkey on his plate. I rolled my eyes. I guess it was better she play the part of the loving wife as compared to causing trouble. I prayed they could make it through dinner without either of them showing their behind. The doorbell rang, breaking into my thoughts.

"I'll get it," Wesleigh yelled out.

Seeing my sister smiling and not scowling this Christmas was heartwarming. Looking around at my family enjoying each other, I was content in knowing the day was almost over and I hadn't caused any drama. Six more hours to go, and I could officially say I won Christmas.

# Chapter 18

I turned toward the doorway as I heard the excitement of Wesleigh and her guest greeting one another. I walked over to see who the surprise guest was and introduce myself.

"Hey, girl. Merry Christmas. Come on in." She pulled her friend in for a warm embrace.

As they separated and I saw her friend's face, a lump formed in my throat.

She extended her hand for her to come inside. I took a few steps backward, wishing I could be further away from them all. Wesleigh turned toward me, and I knew it was too late to run now.

"Meeghan, this is my sister—"

"Harper? So good to see you again," she exclaimed. "I met her at the airport the other day. Did she tell you? She sat next to Felix on her flight."

"No, no she didn't mention it. Small world."

I responded with a weak wave. "Yes, great to see you again. Make yourself at home. The kitchen is to the right. Uh...I'm sure Wesleigh will show you where to go."

I tried not to look in Wesleigh's direction, but I could see the worry lines creasing her forehead out of the corner of my eye.

"No problem at all. Right this way."

"Oh wait...my fiancé is parking the car."

"No worries. Harper can bring him to the kitchen to join us. Right, Harper?"

My mouth dropped open, but I managed to nod. I couldn't find any words. Wesleigh's brows shot up, but she didn't ask any questions. So much for a quiet Christmas. Things were indeed about to get crazy. Talk about an awkward moment. I needed a drink.

I heard the door push open, and turned to see a smiling Felix.

"What a pleasant surprise." He looked around, and reached in for a hug. "Um, I take it our agreement has remained confidential."

He pulled away and looked into my eyes.

"Oh I haven't said anything to anyone, but as you know, the truth always finds a way of coming out." In a hushed voice, I said, "And if I were you, I might find a reason to not be here."

He grimaced, not sure what I meant by my statement, but as soon as we entered the kitchen, it all came together.

"Everyone this is Felix Stapleton, Meeghan's fiancé. He's a scout for the Atlanta Falcons, Daddy."

My father gave a thumbs up. "Now this is a man I can get along with. Sir, come on over and let me fix you something to drink."

I was in the corner of the room, hidden among the sea of aunts, uncles, cousins, friends, and extended family. I zeroed in on Terri, and she was scowling something serious. I shifted my gaze to Felix, and he looked about as comfortable as one of America's most wanted at a police convention.

"If you don't mind, I'll walk with you to get that drink," Felix offered.

I didn't blame him for wanting to leave the kitchen. It was definitely hot in there and it wasn't from the ovens. Poor Meeghan was clueless. I hoped Terri wasn't ready to fill her in.

"This house is lovely, Mrs. Hilson, and your daughters are wonderful. I've only just met Harper, but she's super sweet."

"Thank you, Meeghan. And you said you work out at Wesleigh's gym?"

She bobbed her head. "Yep. Been working out there for about six months now. She's helping me get ready for the big day," Meeghan announced, holding up her ring.

My mouth hadn't left the floor and my eyes had to be the size of the moon by now. This did not go unnoticed by Donovan.

He leaned in to whisper, "What the heck is wrong with you? You look spooked. You know them?"

I shook my head. "Nah. I met them at the airport the other day and we exchanged info. I helped him put an offer down on a house."

Donovan rubbed his hands together. "Oh, ok cool. And he a scout for the Falcons, huh? Well shoot, make sure you tell him to holler at me when he needs a new whip."

When I didn't respond, Donovan nudged me.

"Did the deal with the house not work out? What the heck is going on up there?" He pointed toward my head. "You need to tell me something?"

I opened my mouth to speak, and closed it again. Lord knows I would love to tell him what I knew, but that would make this scenario more real than I cared to accept at the moment. Besides, I wanted my family to be able to enjoy Christmas free from drama and inviting him into this could only make matters worse. I had to find Keesa.

He placed his hand on my shoulder. "Look, whatever it is, you can tell me and I'm not going to trip out on you."

I pursed my lips. "It's not anything *you* should get mad at me about anyway, but thanks. I'll holler at you in a bit."

I walked over and tapped Keesa on the shoulder. "Hey, I need to speak with you about a *business* matter. Real quick."

Keesa raised a brow. She must have seen the hint of panic I was trying to hide. She excused herself and followed me to the garage where a few card games were underway.

"What's up? I don't like that look. Looks like the 'we lost money' look. What's going on?"

"So the guy I met at the airport, Felix. He's here as Wesleigh's guest with his fiancé, Meeghan. Oh, and Terri—his mistress—is here with her husband. I'm sure he's purchasing that home for Terri since she showed up to view it. This is a mess."

"Goodness. Okay, calm down, and let's think about this." Keesa chewed on her thumbnail. "I really think you're making a big deal out of this, Harper. As long as the side chick knows her place, then there shouldn't be a problem, and considering nothing has popped off yet, I doubt anything will."

I inhaled and exhaled. She was right. I was driving myself crazy and it was unnecessary worry.

"True. Okay, I need to relax my mind. Let's go back inside. I think I need some more of the naughty nog."

"Cheers to the nog," Keesa said, raising her glass.

Keesa and I walked back into the house. We exchanged glances, hers to reassure me it would be fine and mine to tell her things had to be fine. However, judging from the energy in the room, the calm before the storm was just about over.

# Chapter 19

Walking into the family room, the first thing I noticed was Terri had moved closer to where Felix and Meeghan were standing. They were in a group talking with Wesleigh, and a few of my cousins. Jabari was watching football and playing cards across the room with Kwesi, oblivious to what was going on across the room.

It was in my best interest to stay away from any conversation that included Meeghan, Felix, or Terri. Terri was feverishly stirring her drink, her eyes transitioning from Meeghan's ring finger to Felix's face. From the look on Wesleigh's face, I believe she may have detected some tension. As much as I wanted to stay out of their business, I thought it might be worth it for me to discuss this with my brother and sister.

"Keesa, can you go join their conversation and try to maintain order? I need to pull Donovan and Wesleigh to the side for a minute."

She nodded. "Good 'cause we might need reinforcements. I'm on it, girl."

Keesa and I walked over to join the group just as Terri was starting her interrogation on the status of Felix and Meeghan's relationship.

"Sorry to interrupt your dissertation on love for this man, but how did y'all two meet, Melissa?" Terri spewed.

"Actually, it's Meeghan and we met in college. We both went to Auburn University. He was on the football team, and I was the Residence Director for the dorm where he stayed. We reconnected at an alumni game, and the rest is history."

Terri folded her arms over her chest. "Oh, how *cute*, Morgan." She feigned a yawn. "Such a *sweet* story. Does anyone else have anything more *interesting* to share?"

Meeghan shook her head and smirked. "Did I miss something? I don't recall doing anything to offend you."

Terri took a sip from her cup. "Your presence here was enough," she mumbled before walking away.

I grabbed Wesleigh by the elbow and pulled her away.

"Why are you grabbing my arm? With the way Terri is acting, I don't think we need to go too far."

"I know, and she's part of the reason I need to talk to you."

Wesleigh stopped walking and stood directly in front of me.

"What the heck is going on, Harper?"

Placing my hands on my hips, I said, "Once we get Donovan, I'll tell you both at the same time. I'd rather do this once. We might need all hands on deck if this goes sideways."

Pretending to shoot herself in the head, Wesleigh whined, "What did you do now?"

"Whoa, I didn't do anything," I said. "Dang, Wessy."

"What's up?" Donovan said, walking up behind us. "I saw Keesa and she told me to find y'all."

I quickly rehashed the details on how I first met Felix and Meeghan, and linked up with Felix for the property viewing only to discover he and Terri were having a fling.

"You know what? Terri is toying with danger, Honey." Wesleigh snorted. "Meeghan is sweet, but she ain't weak."

Donovan was speechless. "That's jacked up. Jabari is in there sick over her, and she all in ol' girl face being fake."

"For the record, I want to point out that I didn't invite Jabari, Terri, Felix, or Meeghan to the house. And, I didn't tell anyone about the other. I minded my business per my family's recommendation. Now…what are we going to do?"

I felt a tap on my shoulder.

"Hey, you got a minute?" Jabari asked.

"Um, sure." I looked back at my siblings. "How long have you been standing there, by the way?"

"Just walked up. Had to get out of there. I needed to get some air. I'll meet you outside," I heard Jabari say.

I looked at Donovan and then over at Wesleigh. "What do you think? Should I tell him what's going on? He deserves a heads up."

"No, don't tell him anything, yet."

"Keep him occupied outside, while we figure out a way to get Felix and Meeghan out of the house," Wesleigh added. "They were only supposed to stay for a quick visit anyway. I'll see what I can do."

Knowing the situation was under control, I walked out back to meet with Jabari. I knew this was probably not a good idea, but it wasn't like I didn't have family filling every crevice of this house. It wasn't like we were going to be alone and booed up—it was a quick chat between friends.

* * *

Jabari stood against the frame of the garage. I was glad to see my cousins were still outside playing cards and now someone had pulled out the dominoes, too. They were in a heated competition by now. The shake of the table could be heard in the night air as someone slammed down a bone and yelled out, "Domino".

"I can't believe Terri showed up here," he said, as soon as I got within earshot. "Kwesi must have mentioned your mom invited us over."

"It looked like you two were getting along earlier. Are you open to working this out?"

Jabari shook his head and exhaled. I could smell that he had taken a dive in the naughty nog pool. Or perhaps he went straight to the bourbon. Either way his

118

breath was letting me know truth serum was on tap tonight.

"Terri ain't trying to look bad—she's trying to put up a front." He shook his head, taking another sip from his cup before speaking again. "I'm never going to be enough for her. Never going to provide her with the life she thinks she deserves."

I sighed. "What makes you think that? Did she actually say those words to you?"

"Her friend's husband got a job making more money, which got Terri to thinking I didn't make enough to provide for us." He took a sip from his red solo cup. "Did you see the way she was salivating over ol' boy? I guess when she heard someone say he was a scout for the Falcons, that got her libido up and going."

My lips twisted, but they didn't part with the truth. I thought this was the perfect segue to tell him everything, but if Wesleigh and Donovan were able to get Felix and Meeghan to leave, we could let them figure their love triangle out on their own time.

"Well Jabari, I'm not sure if you all have really sat down and talked about this, but she's really the one you should speak with and not me. Have you tried to talk to her?"

He managed to chuckle. "No, not really. She's belittling me every chance she gets. Asking why I don't make more bank. Telling me I need to man up and do more to take care of our home."

I tilted my head and frowned. I could've responded and told him my thoughts. I believed his job was noble and helping to build young minds was a thankless job—and he should feel proud. But that wasn't the role I needed to play in his life. I needed to be a friend and listen. If I wanted to be there for him, it had to be as a listening ear.

While I didn't think Terri had a kind bone in her body, I was swallowing my nasty thoughts and trying to be kind for his sake. "I'm sure she believes in you. You've been together all these years. There's got to be love there."

"Not like the love you used to have for me, though. Do you still have anything in there for me?"

Jabari leaned in for a kiss, and I pushed him back just as Terri came busting through the back door carrying a drink with a side of attitude.

"I knew I would find you with her," Terri shouted. The contents of her drink spilled out from the impact of her glass slamming down on a nearby table. "Trying to get that ol' thang back huh, Bari?"

"I would call this unbelievable, but it's not…and you," Terri said, pointing her finger at me. "You couldn't wait. Talking about you don't know what's going on with us. Liar. Go 'head and tell 'im. Tell everything."

"Whoa." I threw up my hands in defense. "Jabari asked to talk and I'm just here listening. I don't have anything to say about what's going on with you both.

Y'all need to work it out—across the street—at Jabari's house. Not here. Take that drama across the street."

Terri nodded. I exhaled. Glad they knew I wasn't going to be a part of this mess—or so I thought.

"I ought to drag ya lil' bald head behind around this garage." Terri reeled her hand back and smacked me across the face.

I fell backward into Jabari's arms. I touched my face and sent up a prayer of forgiveness. Sunday school lessons weren't going to keep me back this time.

"You done messed up now, trick," I spat.

*Forgive me, Lord.* I lunged toward her, tackling her to the ground.

"WORLDSTAR!"

We rolled around, knocking over what I knew to be the card table and someone's beverage because my back was now wet. I could hear the sound of feet shuffling and a few curse words—probably my own at this point. After a moment, I guess the men stopped spectating and pulled us apart.

"What the heck is going on?" my father demanded.

I cringed in shame. I could've been the bigger person and not retaliated, but she'd had that coming for years. And well, it was self-defense. She came for me first. I dropped my head. We were too grown for this.

"Sorry, Dad. Go back inside. *Terri*, Jabari, and I will clean this up." I looked around at my nosey cousins. "Why don't y'all go get some dessert and give us a second to clean up? Oh, and whoever talking about sending this to Worldstar, don't even think about it."

"I told you not to yell it out, fool. Shoo, we could've got all the likes and hella follows off that one," I heard one of my cousins say.

They left at a turtle's pace, trying to catch a few more words in our heated exchange, but I didn't say anything to the odd couple until all was clear. I turned to face the two, but my mouth dropped when a third person emerged from the side of the house.

"Charles? Oh my gosh. Baby, what are you doing here?" I shook my head. Even though I saw him standing there, I was in disbelief. "When did you get here?"

Seeing the stunned expression on his face, I knew I must have looked a hot mess. I combed my fingers through my hair and pulled out some grass.

"What the heck happened here?"

He gawked at the card tables laying on the ground, scattered plates of food, and the broken bottles in the driveway and front lawn. It looked as if someone had dumped a bag of trash in the yard.

I exhaled. "You don't even want to know…are those for me?" I pointed to the dozen roses held loosely at his side.

"Oh, yeah. I forgot I had them. Are you okay?"

I closed my eyes as his hand stroked the side of my face. "Yeah. I'm fine. I'm so happy you're here."

My breath caught as he leaned down to kiss me on the lips

"Um, you've got to be kidding me? I know you see us still standing here."

I rolled my eyes and turned toward Terri. "Why are y'all still here?" I spat.

"Baby, what the heck is going on?" Charles asked. "You got scrapes on your face and nature in your hair." He looked back and forth between me and Terri.

"I guess you supposed to be her man, huh? Chuck, was it?" Terri said, while getting closer to us. "Well you should know your skanky little girlfriend was out here trying to get with my husband," she proclaimed. Holding up her ashy ring finger. "Homewrecker."

I waved her words away. "First of all...last I heard you don't have a home to wreck, and—"

"Second of all, you wrote the standard operating procedures on skank-like tactics...Don't think I didn't know you've been sniffing around my man. He told me everything." Meeghan moved toward us with Felix close on her heels.

That certainly sobered Jabari up.

"Wait, so you're the dude she's been with for the last six months?"

Meeghan nodded. "Yep. He's the one. They messed around a time or two. She thought he was going to leave me for her, but she couldn't be more wrong."

Terri clapped her hands together. "Here...we... go. That shows how much you know. He put money down on a house for us on yesterday."

"What?" Meeghan screeched. "Felix, you had better explain yourself right now."

Felix stammered. "Uh, Baby... you know good and well I ain't paying that broad no attention. I put a ring on your pretty little finger, and she ain't worth losing you. Now come on, Baby."

I felt like we were at a tennis match. Our heads motioned from left to right as the curse words, and accusations flew from every direction.

"Oh I'm a broad now? I got you," Terri yelled, flinging her heel in his direction. And she was a good shot too. The shoe made direct contact with Felix's upper lip.

Holding his mouth he mumbled, "Meeghan, why don't we get in the car and talk about this later? No need to disrupt this family gathering."

I nodded, rushing to push Felix and Meeghan in the direction where the cars were parked. "That's a great idea. Why don't you all take those conversations home? They're private and shouldn't be wasted on us here."

As Felix begged and pleaded with Meeghan on their way to the car, Terri clicked her teeth and set her sights back on Jabari.

"Ugh, I'm so over this whole situation. Bari, let's go. Ain't nobody thinking about Harper or that ol' Green Mile looking fool." She moved closer to him, pressing her breasts against his chest. "Baby, I'm sorry. Can I come back home?"

Jabari pulled Terri into a warm embrace, kissed her on the cheeks, and said, "Man, heck nah. I'm out." He chucked the deuces in Terri's face. "Harp, thanks for everything. Tell Kwesi I'm gone."

As Jabari crossed the street, Terri jogged behind him, clearly not willing to take no for an answer.

Charles and I exchanged a glance, and started toward the house.

"Welcome to Christmas with the Hilsons. We host fights every week and twice on the weekends." I chuckled solemnly. "This is not quite what I had in mind for the first time you spent Christmas with me and my family."

He stopped walking and turned me to him, softly raking his fingers through my hair. "You sure you're okay?" Charles fussed.

"Yes, I'm fine, baby. Your being here is a major factor in that."

Charles took my hand and kissed the tips of my fingers. "Sorry it took me so long to get here."

Looking into his eyes, I felt the words he'd spoken had a much deeper meaning. Only time would tell, but I was hoping this meant from here on out, I wouldn't have to celebrate Christmas or any other holiday without him.

Walking back into the house, I had forgotten I was in a miniature brawl until my father came over with an ice pack.

"Put this on your face, Baby Girl. It looks like you might be safe from a black eye, but your cheek is red."

"Charles, you showed up just in time to see Sugar Ray Harper in the ring," Donovan teased.

Charles cupped his hand across his mouth, trying to muffle his laughter.

"Very funny, Donnie. Why don't you make yourself useful and show Charles where to grab a plate of food."

I took the ice bag from my father, and placed it against my cheek. "Thanks, Daddy. I'm really sorry about making a scene and I know—"

He held up his hands. "No need to apologize. It's not like you invited them over here," he said, setting eyes on my mother. We shared a laugh. "Why don't you go freshen up?"

I nodded and kissed my father on the cheek before heading to the guest bathroom in the hallway. As soon as I saw my face, I groaned. I turned my head to the side to examine the severity, and much like my father said, I saw the beginnings of a bruise. I checked my eye and while it looked puffy, there didn't appear to be any damage there. I would check again tomorrow.

My makeup was smudged from all the tussling. I wet a wash cloth from the linen closet and dabbed my face. I wasn't going to bother to reapply the makeup. At this point, everyone knew there had been an altercation outside and that I was involved. It was what it was.

I walked out of the bathroom just in time to hear a knock at the door. I inhaled deeply. I couldn't take any more surprises tonight. I hadn't even gotten a chance to get any dessert. Screw the door. I got some banana pudding with my name on it. Come to think of, I hadn't had much to eat either. It'd been a long day."

I started toward the kitchen when my cousin Ronald called out to me.

"Ay cuzzo, it's somebody at the do'. Want me to let her in?"

I walked over to the door and smiled. "Hey Paula, Merry Christmas."

# Chapter 20

I closed the door behind her and looked over my shoulder to see where Donovan could be. He would be happy she came. It was getting late, and I had forgotten she said she might come through.

"Merry Christmas to you, too. Um, sorry to stare, but what happened to you?"

"You don't even want to know." I bowed my head. "Anyway, Donovan is around here somewhere. Make yourself at home and I'll find him for you."

Paula looked in the direction of the living room. "If you don't mind, I don't want to create a scene, though he did invite me. With everything that happened last time—it was awkward with your parents—and how I left everything. I'll just wait right here."

I nodded. I walked into the living room to see if Donovan had taken Charles in there to watch football, and sure enough, that's exactly where he was posted up.

Donovan's breath caught when he saw Paula and Olivia standing in the hallway. As I began to back away and leave them to their moment, Donovan called out to me.

"Harper, can you take Olivia over to where the kids are? I want to have a chat with Paula—alone."

I looked down and smiled at Olivia. It was amazing how much she had grown in a year. The chubby little girl I remembered was starting to stretch out. I took Olivia's hand and led her to the den where the kids were watching *A Christmas Story*—one of my favorites. I walked back down the hall and into the kitchen.

I looked around at the aftermath of Christmas dinner. People were leaning back in chairs rubbing their bellies. A few buttons had been loosened, and everyone had gotten their fill. I reviewed the remains of the buffet line which once displayed full trays of food and desserts. As expected, the sweets had been run through.

There was a corner of pecan pie, some jagged edge slices of chocolate cake, and a half scoop of banana pudding. I went over to the fridge and almost cried when I saw someone took the time to put foil on my plate from earlier. *Thank you Lord.*

Donovan and Paula passed by the kitchen entrance on their way to the family room, it looked like things were going well. She cradled his face and he appeared to be enjoying the attention as evident by the way he leaned into her.

Though today was eventful in a way I couldn't have imagined, I'm so glad it ended the way it did. With my family and my man all together in one place. I couldn't wait to wrap my arms around him and tell him how much I loved him, but first we needed to talk—no better time than now.

# Chapter 21

I was about to go grab Charles from the family room where he was playing Dominoes, when Wesleigh walked into the kitchen. She smiled and shook her head. I nodded because I knew she was about to clown me.

She clapped her hands slowly and then picked up the pace. "Harp, it's close to midnight and you managed to not get in anyone's business—*directly*. I think that's something to celebrate," Wesleigh joked.

"Tell that to my jaw. Today has been crazy, but you're right. I can hold my head high and say the drama we experienced this time around was not my doing."

Donovan joined us in the kitchen.

"Amen. This has been a great Christmas for all of us. I'm meeting with Olivia and Paula to go ice skating tomorrow."

I reached for him and pulled him into a bear hug. "Donnie...I knew you would get a heart for Christmas...you big Grinch you."

"Whatever. You know those two are my heart. Now, get up off me and get up on my man here." He nodded in the direction where Charles was standing.

"Come on, Wessy. Let's let these two talk now that the circus has left."

Wesleigh chuckled. "I do recall seeing a few clowns earlier. Let's go, Big Brother."

I didn't know what it was about all the chaos of the day, but in that moment, seeing Charles made everything better.

Looking down at me, he examined my face again before kissing me on the lips. "So who are we suing?"

I shook my head. "No need to take it there, but if it pleases the court, I would like to present Exhibit A." I put my hand over my heart.

"Oh that's what I'm talking about, but we might need to get a room."

I swatted at his arm. "No silly, Exhibit A is my heart. I want to present my heart to you completely. I love you so much, but I'd be lying if I didn't say every year on Christmas, there's been a bit of a blockage."

He rubbed his goatee and nodded. "I can see that. You do tend to get a bit distant around this time of year."

"This is my favorite holiday, and every year you spend it with your firm. I know you want me there with you, as you're trying to become partner and I want you here with me. I've never really expressed how important it is for me to have you here, so I don't blame you for not knowing. I was focused on being supportive and held my tongue on what I needed from you. I knew my tone would come across wrong because I waited too long to express

131

myself — and by doing so, I allowed myself to get upset with you when I should've told you how I was feeling."

Charles frowned. "That's not fair to our relationship if I'm only telling you what I need and want. You can't be afraid to speak up. I need to know what you need."

I laid my head on his chest. "It's funny. In my personal life, I seldom speak up for what I want for me. But whenever it's someone else's life, I have no problem with telling them what they need to do. I stay in somebody else's business."

He laughed. "But Ms. Hilson, I've been trying to make you my business full-time for years. You could've inserted your two cents and told me what you wanted me to do."

My eyes widened. "So you're saying if I had told you I wanted you to be here and stopping putting the partners first…you would've honored my request?"

He groaned. "I thought something might be wrong, but you never said anything so I proceeded per usual. But at the end of the day, I'm your man and I don't have any plans to change that. Now tell me what you want, and let's try to make some progress in our relationship."

I nodded. "Okay, since I have the floor—I want you to find some work-life balance. I want you to give us as much time as you put into trying to become partner. This relationship has billable hours too—we have to invest in us. No one else is going to do that for us—we have to work on this together."

He leaned down and kissed me on my forehead. "You're right and I apologize for being self-absorbed and missing moments that were important to you—to us. I love you and I want you to be happy."

"And I want you to be happy too, but we have to be in this together and I have to feel like I can ask you anything and tell you anything."

"Agreed. Now let me say this, I might not always be able to fulfill your requests—but I want to spend the rest of my life trying."

Unable to contain my happiness, I said, "Well…if you're asking me to tell you it's time to change my last name to Mendoza…then I must say, I think it's time I changed my last name."

"So you mean to tell me you were the hold up from me getting a new son-in-law?" My mother sucked her teeth. "I told you to speak up and tell him what you need. Got time to be in your brother and sister affairs, but can't talk to your man. Oh Harper? Really? Charles, I'm so sorry our daughter don't have enough sense to see a good man in front of her."

My father came into the kitchen. "What's going on now?"

"From the sound of it—Chuck wants to marry Harper and she was too busy in everybody else business to handle her own business."

My mouth gaped open, but Charles was unbothered by the whole exchange. As they went back and forth about what I was and wasn't doing—he was seizing the moment.

"Well...since I know loving you means coming with the unexpected, I've been keeping this ring in my jacket pocket...patiently waiting for the right opportunity to show you just how much I love you. Now in front of my nosey future-in-laws and God, I want to know if you, Harper Hilson, will be my wife."

"Ah—hellll, nah. You ain't even gonna drop to one knee? You too young to not be able to drop to ya' knee. That's what's wrong with these young fellas," Uncle LaFayette said.

"Hush, he was about to kneel, weren't you Charles?" my mother asked while dabbing her eyes.

As my family went back and forth on how the proposal should go, I allowed myself to enjoy the moment and get closer to the man I loved.

Wrapping my arms around his neck, I whispered into his ear, "I swear this family is crazy. You sure you want to be a part of this?"

"If you'll give me the chance—I want this crazy forever."

"Then I guess you better ice me up. I would absolutely love to marry you."

"SHE SAID YES," my mother squealed.

"WORLDSTER," my father yelled.

"Mama, get your husband. And it's Worldstar, Daddy," I exclaimed as Charles guffawed once again.

"Andrew, go sit down somewhere," my mother demanded.

"All right, all right. Can't do jack around here. Merry Christmas to y'all, too.

Learning into Charles chest, my heart was full. Being back in a good place with my siblings, and finally being ready to take this journey... it was indeed a Merry Christmas and the new year ahead wasn't looking too bad either. I guess more than Christmas bells would be ringing for this family.

Thank you for reading Bells Will Be Ringin'

## Continue reading for an excerpt of

# Kissing Strangers

Coming February 2018

# Chapter 1

## Brittain

It was a beautiful day for a jog. For the last three years, running was the one constant in my life. One of my girlfriends convinced me to join a national running group called Black Girls Run. It was an amazing network of women and was a needed addition to my hectic world.

Pulling my sisterlocks into a high bun, I trotted over to a park bench to do some stretching before I began my trek. Piedmont Park was really busy today. People walked. People jogged. *People*…that looked a lot like my fiancé, Kenneth—had picnics. *Picnics*…with another woman that sure as *heck* ain't me.

My first instinct was to walk over and investigate the situation, but I decided that I needed to do a little more investigating from afar. They looked very familiar with each other. She gently stroked his cheek while he fed her strawberries—that level of familiarity. Sitting in between his legs, with her head against his chest—type of familiar. Yeah, that was enough discovery for me, this was exactly what it looked like.

I walked up the hill slowly, trying to maintain my composure because everyone knows you don't want to look like a crazed woman when confronting the man that you're supposed to marry. Those were my intentions to just talk to him, but my right hand going across the back of his head had another theory.

"Ouch—what the heck?!" he yelled grabbing the back of his head. "—oh snap, Brit?! Uh-uh. Hey baby—uh, what you doing out here?"

"Kenny, what the heck is this?" I growled, pointing towards the chick who had yet to budge from in between his legs. "And don't disrespect me with a lie because I hardly think you would be feeding fruit to a cousin, sister, or auntie." Brittain paused, planting her once flailing hands on her hips. "So what is this?"

"First of all, you should really calm down—*considering*... that I'm his wife and you're his side chick," she spat, rising to her feet. "I knew he was having an affair, but clearly you've lost your mind and forgot your place. Kenneth, you really need to teach your women to learn to respect the woman affording you to take them on lavish trips and four-star restaurants," she barked.

My eyes blinked rapidly, as I looked from Kenneth back to the woman claiming to be his rib. "Your wife? So you ask me to marry you and you're already married?" I said, looking at them both and holding up my left hand.

This time it was his wife that was ready to explode. I stood there and watched as she lunged across their beautiful picnic spread and pummeled him the way that I should have been.

"You proposed to her? You idiot! What were you thinking?"

He threw up his hands to protect his face from the blows. "June, stop it! The ring doesn't mean anything. I made vows to you," he proclaimed, trying to regain some control. "Besides it's that costume jewelry stuff."

Looking down at the ring, I slid it off my finger, and I tossed it at his head. *There, I got one shot in,* I thought to myself as I realized my true love was nothing more than unnecessary trouble.

As a crowd began to form around the tussling twosome, I walked away—gradually building up my speed and doing what I did best—jogging out my worries.

24302772R00078

Made in the USA
Columbia, SC
20 August 2018